"It's a very big deal for a girl from the Texas boonies to ask a man for a date,"

she said when he picked her up. "I hope you realize that."

"I kind of figured it out," he said with a grin.

"What tipped you off?"

"You sounded a little breathless," he said cheerfully. "Like you couldn't get the words out."

"I was that bad?"

"Don't worry. It's kind of nice to have the shoe on the other foot. Every time a man calls a woman up for a date he's nervous. We're all actors. Inside, we're a mass of quivering jelly."

She cast him a blatantly skeptical look. "Forgive me, but I don't believe you. I'm not sure I've ever met anyone who's more self-confident than you."

What could he say? She was right.

Dear Reader,

When two people fall in love, the world is suddenly new and exciting, and it's that same excitement we bring to you in Silhouette Intimate Moments. These are stories with scope, with grandeur. The characters lead the lives we all dream of, and everything they do reflects the wonder of being in love.

Longer and more sensuous than most romances, Silhouette Intimate Moments novels take you away from everyday life and let you share the magic of love. Adventure, glamour, drama, even suspense—these are the passwords that let you into a world where love has a power beyond the ordinary, where the best authors in the field today create stories of love and commitment that will stay with you always.

In coming months look for novels by your favorite authors: Maura Seger, Parris Afton Bonds, Linda Howard and Nora Roberts, to name just a few. And whenever you buy books, look for all the Silhouette Intimate Moments, love stories *for* today's women *by* today's women.

Leslie J. Wainger
Senior Editor
Silhouette Books

Maura Seger
Day and Night

Silhouette Intimate Moments
Published by Silhouette Books New York

America's Publisher of Contemporary Romance

SILHOUETTE BOOKS
300 East 42nd St., New York, N.Y. 10017

Copyright © 1988 by Maura Seger

ISBN: 0-373-07224-4

First Silhouette Books printing January 1988

America's Publisher of Contemporary Romance

Printed in the U.S.A.

MAURA SEGER

was prompted by a love of books and a vivid imagination to decide, at age twelve, to be a writer. Twenty years later her first book was published. So much, she says, for overnight success! Now each book is an adventure, filled with fascinating people who always surprise her.

Chapter 1

There was something to be said for coming into money when one was still young enough to enjoy it, but old enough not to take it for granted.

Or so Cara Herrington reflected as she walked home from work through Central Park early one fall evening. It was still light enough for her to clearly see the sentinel-like towers that ringed the greensward. Depending on the light, they seemed to alternately threaten or protect it. Just then the effect was oddly comforting. Oddly, because there had been a time when she'd believed she would never feel at home in New York. Now she couldn't imagine living elsewhere.

The glamorous, exciting, unexpectedly charming city suited her. With her tall, leggy body, her casually styled blond hair and her elegant good looks, she fit right into the rarefied circles in which she moved. The fact that she still often felt like an interloper didn't seem to matter to anyone except her.

With a sigh, she dug her hands into the pockets of her russet suede jacket and picked up her pace. It was getting chillier, and the light was fading quickly. She might still be a novice to New York, but she wasn't foolish enough to be in a lonely part of the park after dark.

A woman passed her going in the opposite direction. She was pushing a stroller in which a sleepy three-year-old lolled. For a moment, the woman's eyes met Cara's. Both smiled. The innocence of a child was one of the few things that could overcome the barriers most city dwellers automatically erected.

That was something she would never get used to. Back home in Texas people were friendlier, at least when they weren't busy spreading rumors. She'd had more than her fair share of gossip back when she was too young, too poor and too proud to defend herself. No more. Now she had everything money could buy, except that she simply didn't want most of it. The freedom, though, was another matter. She liked being able to do work she loved, rather than taking a job simply to put food on the table. Perhaps the greatest luxury in the world was to be able to make a difference.

She turned eastward and saw in the distance the glint of fading light on the reservoir. The path that ran around it was a favorite spot for joggers, and several of them were taking their laps as she walked closer.

The path cut through a copse of magnolia trees, their twisted branches almost bare of leaves. Their gnarled trunks cast long shadows that made her shiver slightly.

Afterward, she wondered if there hadn't been the briefest instant of premonition, a forewarning of danger she'd had neither the time nor the reflexes to heed. At the moment, she was only aware of a slight rustling in the trees to her left, a sudden rush of movement, and the pressure of a hard hand over her mouth and nose, cutting off her breath.

Cara screamed, but no sound escaped. The man who held her was very strong. Though she clawed at his arm frantically, he did not even begin to loosen his grip. Distantly, she became aware of another man alongside them. She had the vague impression that he was young, slender, impatient and nervous.

"Come on," she heard him mutter hoarsely. "Get her out of sight."

Inexorably, she was dragged backward toward a thick clump of bushes that would effectively screen her from all eyes.

Terror doubled and redoubled within her. How stupid could she be, not to have heeded the warnings of people who said it was dangerous for a woman to walk alone at any time. How stubbornly she had refused to give in to that kind of fear, only to be confronted by one even more real and horrifying.

Did they intend only to rob her? That was undoubtedly the best she could hope for. Realistically, she knew they might intend far worse. Mere thieves would have seized her purse and kept right on going, instead of deliberately waylaying her. A sickening sense of violation spread through her even at the thought of what they might intend. Was she to become a victim of one of those assaults she noticed regularly on the nightly news and tried to ignore? A paralyzing numbness began to spread over her, as

though her mind was trying to prepare her for what
was to come.

They had reached the bushes. The man holding her
laughed harshly as he lowered her onto the ground,
still covering her mouth with his hand. He had slid it
down low enough to let her breathe, but that was in no
way reassuring. Especially not when he bent over her
and she saw that he, like his cohort, was masked.

"Real pretty," the first man said. "You a model,
honey?"

She made no attempt to answer, nor did he seem to
expect any. He merely laughed again and slid a hand
under her jacket. "Nice."

Something snapped inside Cara. Heedless of her
own safety, she lashed out, giving no thought to anything except stopping what she was now certain the
men intended to do. Her sharp teeth dug into her as-
sailant's hand, drawing blood. When he instinctively
yanked it away, she screamed with all her might, even
as she endeavored to scramble to her feet.

She almost made it, and indeed might have, if the
other man hadn't recovered swiftly from his surprise
and reached out for her. He grabbed her suede jacket
and was dragging her back into the bushes when suddenly, without warning, she was free.

Lying stunned on the ground, she was aware of a
series of dull thuds and grunts, interspersed with what
could only be described as highly colorful cursing. The
struggle could not have lasted more than a few moments before a hand touched her shoulder.

Cara stiffened and opened her mouth to scream
again, only to be stopped by a low, gentle voice. "It's
okay, you're safe now. Take it easy." Strong arms
lifted her, and she was cradled against a broad chest.

Her rescuer, whoever he was, carried her out of the bushes, to a bench a short distance away. He set her down gently.

"I have to call this in," he said. "The police phone is right there." He gestured toward a nearby pole that had a metal box attached to it. "You'll be okay for a moment?"

Numbly, Cara nodded. She was still struggling to catch her breath and come to terms with what had almost happened to her. It seemed as though no more than seconds passed before her rescuer returned and bent down in front of her.

"There'll be a squad car here in a couple of minutes. You okay to talk?"

"Yes . . . I think so. Thank you. I don't know what I would have done if you hadn't . . ."

"Don't think about it," the man said brusquely. He moved a little closer, and she found herself staring into coal-black eyes. His hair was ebony, cut short and curling tightly over a well-shaped head. He looked about eight or so years older than her twenty-seven years. His face was square, with rugged features and a tan that looked as though it had been acquired in hard outdoor work rather than at some resort.

Only then did she become aware of how he was dressed: in gray stretch pants and a sweatshirt, both of which had definitely seen better days, possibly several decades ago. The shirt had an interesting arrangement of ragged holes and was dark in large areas, suggesting that he had been perspiring heavily.

"I'm Mark Sabatini, by the way," he said. "I'm a cop myself, so when the guys show up, let me handle it."

"Those men . . ."

He cocked his head back toward the bushes. "They aren't going anywhere. Don't worry about it."

Her eyes widened as a sudden possibility occurred to her. "You didn't . . . ?"

"Do what I would have liked to them? No, I'm not in the habit of taking the law into my own hands. But I can tell you they aren't going to be feeling any too good for a while." He reached out a hand and touched her cheek lightly. "It looks as though they deserved everything they got, and more."

Cara suddenly became aware that her body throbbed painfully from head to toe. She winced, envisioning what she must look like under her clothes. But then she thought of how much worse it might have been, and a small, brave smile lifted the corners of her mouth.

Mark watched it, entranced. Not until he had dealt with her attackers had he begun to notice anything about her other than the most obvious details. Describing her as "white, female, midtwenties, five-feet-five-inches, one hundred and twenty pounds, eyes blue, hair blond," did not begin to get close to the reality.

The only other words he could think of to describe her—knockout, gorgeous, a "10"—didn't seem appropriate either because they missed an intrinsic quality, which he recognized but didn't quite know what to call. Finally, he decided that she simply looked like a lady. A very beautiful, somewhat delicate, and still rather fearful one.

The instinctive protectiveness that was so much a part of his nature surged to the fore. He had to fight down the impulse to go back into the bushes and finish off the two creeps lying there. The mere idea of their hands on her filled him with disgust and rage.

"What is it?" Cara whispered, her gaze frozen on him. She had watched the play of emotions over his powerfully masculine face and, while she could not interpret them all correctly, she sensed that he was very, very angry.

"Nothing," he said, standing up abruptly. She followed the long stretch of his body with her eyes, realizing that he was even taller than she had thought. He was over six feet in height and solidly built, with a broad chest and shoulders that tapered down to a firm waist and slender hips. The stretch pants he wore had long since lost their elasticity and were baggy, but even they could not conceal the powerful muscles of his thighs and calves. He was in excellent condition which, she supposed, accounted at least in part for his being able to overcome her assailants.

"You said you're a policeman," she murmured. "Were you on patrol here?" She had heard that the plainclothes detective force had recently been beefed up. Perhaps they were making a special effort to protect the park which, from her recently gained perspective, certainly seemed like a good idea.

But Mark shook his head. "I was jogging. I live over near Columbus, and I like to run some place where there aren't any cars."

Cara knew the area around Columbus Avenue well. Though she lived in the opposite direction—on the east side—she frequently had dinner at one of the seemingly hundreds of exotic little restaurants that had sprung up in what had once been a less than desirable neighborhood. That had all changed with the arrival of the "Yuppies," who had transformed it into a vista of boutiques, specialty stores, high-priced apartments and even higher priced condominiums.

As though he could read her train of thought, Mark said a shade defensively, "I've been living there since I joined the force, going on fifteen years ago."

"A long time," she said, thinking out loud.

He had to agree with her, though he suspected she didn't know the half of it. Being a cop for even a year was tough. Sometimes, when he really thought about the fact that he'd been at it as long as he had, he felt a sense of shock at both the passage of time and his own endurance. It wasn't that anything got easier, although at least he had gotten inured to some things. Still, the day-to-day routine—if never knowing what to expect could be called that—often left him feeling drained.

But then there were times—like now—when he was damn glad that he had the reflexes and the skill to do what he had done.

The wail of a siren brought him upright. He gave her a last, worried glance and headed for the curb. Neither of the two policemen who got out of the car were known to him, but that didn't especially matter. He flashed his badge and nodded his head toward the bushes.

"Two perps, assault and attempted rape. The victim should be able to give a statement, but go easy on her."

The younger of the two men shot him a surprised look. He caught it and flushed slightly. No one had to tell him that there was something unprofessional in his concern for her. Every cop who had been on the job more than a few weeks knew that it was essential to maintain objectivity, if only to stay sane. But every once in a while that proved to be impossible.

He went back over to the bench and sat down next to her. She was looking at the policemen with an expression he saw regularly on the faces of civilians who had little contact with the authorities. It was a kind of puzzlement over how she had come to be involved with them.

One of the officers nodded to her as they both stepped toward the bushes. Mark felt her stiffen as they pulled out their guns.

"It's strictly a precaution," he said. "Standard procedure."

"Sure," Cara said. "I understand."

In a pig's eye, Mark thought. Looking the way she did—all cool and elegant—he was willing to bet she might never have actually seen a gun before except on television. He felt a moment of resentment at such innocence. No wonder she'd been walking alone in the park at that hour. It had probably never even occurred to her that she could end up the victim of a crime.

"You know," he said, "you really should have had more sense than to be here on your own this close to dark."

Cara turned her head and looked at him. Absently, he noticed that her blue eyes had gone suddenly darker. "Are you saying this was my fault?"

"No, of course not," he hastened to assure her. "Only that you have to watch out for yourself. There are a lot of creeps around."

"So I've discovered."

The shakiness of her soft, honeyed voice with its very un-New York accent got to him. Without stopping to think, he put his arm around her and drew her close. "It's okay," he murmured. "You'll forget about this before you know it."

"I don't think so," Cara said. If nothing else, she had just learned an important lesson, namely that her new life did not protect her from the violence she had witnessed in her old one. Poverty bred cruelty, and inevitably that cruelty spilled out in all directions like a river on the rampage.

Mark misunderstood her. He thought she meant that she feared she wouldn't be able to put the attack behind her and get on with her life. That happened sometimes to women who were suddenly confronted with their own vulnerability. In such a case, counseling was a good idea.

"Look," he said, "there are people you can talk to. Maybe they could help."

She shot him a curious glance. "Thanks, but I don't think that will be necessary. After all, I got off very lightly."

Before he could reply, the policemen returned with the handcuffed assailants stumbling between them. Mark accompanied the young cop he had spoken with and saw the two attackers safely stowed in the back seat of the squad car. The policeman asked, "You want the collar?"

Mark shook his head. He had no particular desire to get credit for the arrest. All that would mean to him was more paperwork, of which he already had more than enough. "You take it."

The officer nodded his thanks, then looked at Cara. "She holding up all right?"

"Yes, but I think the sooner this is wrapped up, the better."

While his partner kept an eye on the attackers, the young man went over to the bench. Cara looked up at him calmly. "We'll need to ask you a few questions, Miss."

"I understand."

She could see that her calmness gave him pause, but she held on to her composure with desperate determination. This would all be finished soon, and she would be back in her own apartment, in her own bed. Holding on to that thought, she even managed to give him a slight smile.

He returned it and nodded approvingly. She could see that he was glad not to have a hysterical victim on his hands. "There'll be another car here in a minute," he said. "You and Lieutenant Sabatini can take it over to the station house. We'll meet you there and get your statement."

Cara was dreading having to relive the incident, even verbally, but she gave no sign of her apprehension. Instead, she merely nodded and assured the policeman that he would have her full cooperation. Not until he went back to the car and drove away did she attempt to stand up, only to discover that her legs weren't quite ready to hold her.

Fortunately, Mark had already anticipated this. Once again she felt his strength and protectiveness as he slipped an arm around her waist. "Easy," he said. "You don't have to rush."

"I just want it over with."

"And it will be, soon."

The other squad car had arrived. They got into the back seat as Mark exchanged a few muted words with the policeman and policewoman who had come with it. Cara made no effort to listen. She stared out the

window at the rapidly gathering darkness and con-
centrated on keeping her mind blank.

Mark kept his thoughts to himself during the short
ride to the station house. She was grateful for that, as
she was for the simple comfort of his presence. There
was something solidly reassuring about him, but then
she supposed that went hand-in-hand with his occupation. He struck her as a man who could handle
himself well in any situation.

Barely had she come to this conclusion when she
experienced a slight frisson of surprise at her preoc-
cupation with him. Under the circumstances, it was
hardly remarkable that he had made a considerable
impact on her. But there was more at work here than
simple gratitude. She observed him surreptitiously out
of the corner of her eye. Grimy sweatshirt and all, he
was a very attractive man. Not in the pretty sense of,
say, a male model, but in the solid, real, on-the-level
sense that was all that ever appealed to her anyway.

Distantly she wondered if there was something
wrong with her, to be thinking of such a thing after the
experience she had gone through. Maybe not, since at
least it proved that she remained capable of very positive feelings. If her attackers had stolen that capacity
from her, it would have been worse than just about
anything they could have done, short of taking her
life.

"I suppose," she said as much to break the silence
as for any other reason, "that I'll have to go to
court?"

"For the indictment, yeah, but maybe not after
that."

"Why not?"

He hesitated to tell her, then decided it was better for her to hear it from him. "This will probably be plea-bargained down to a suspended sentence. They'll plead guilty, but they'll walk."

"I see...."

"It shouldn't be that way, I know, but the system doesn't work as well as it ought to." Which was putting it mildly. There were times when he thought that if he had to put up with the system a moment longer, he would pack up his marbles and get out of the game.

"If that's what's going to happen," Cara said, "why should I bother having them charged?" She really wasn't seriously considering walking away from her responsibilities as a citizen, but she was curious to hear what he would have to say, if only because she found his deep, slightly husky voice very pleasant to listen to.

"You can't do that," he insisted. "It'll only encourage them to go out and do it again, and maybe the next person won't be as lucky as you were. Besides, the more charges they pile up, the better chance there is that eventually some judge will throw the book at them."

"You're right," she said when she realized that he was waiting tensely for her answer. "I'll cooperate any way I can."

Mark expelled a sigh of relief, but hard on it came the realization that she could be in for a rough time. "Remember, I'll be there to back you up. After all, I probably got a better look at them than you did."

She smiled, revealing more than a shadow of her usual vibrant self. "But they're my teeth marks on one of those guys."

"You bit him?"

"As hard as I could."

Mark laughed, a sound that began as a low chuckle and ended as a deep guffaw. He'd been right to think she had spirit and wasn't afraid to stand up for herself. Fancy rich girl or not, there was some substance to her.

"Maybe he'll think twice before going after debutantes."

Cara's eyes widened. In the shadows of the back seat, she searched his face for some sign that he was kidding, only to realize that he wasn't. "You're about ten years too late," she said dryly. Silently, she added, not to mention incredibly far off base.

Mark glanced down at her slender hands with perfectly manicured nails that looked as though they had never done a day's work. She wore no rings, which reassured him, but there was a slim gold watch around her wrist—the discreet Cartier signature just visible. On the other wrist she wore a bracelet of woven gold, with a guard chain, which he knew enough to realize meant that the piece was valuable and needed protecting. Like her.

"Look," he said, "when we finish up at the station house, how about I see you home?"

"Thank you, but . . ."

"But what?"

"I really don't want to impose on you," she told him honestly. "You've already done so much."

"Yeah," he agreed, "and I'd hate to see it go to waste if you got hit by a truck or something."

"Now, why," she asked with a smile, "would I go and do that?"

"Because you're in shock. You just don't realize it yet."

"I feel perfectly all right. A little sore here and there, but otherwise okay."

"Then it's delayed shock. Could hit you at any time."

"Oh." She met his eyes, noticing as she did so how absurdly long and luxurious his eyelashes were. "Well . . . we certainly wouldn't want that to happen, would we?"

He shook his head. "Think how the truck driver would feel."

"It would probably ruin his day."

"What's left of it at least. It's getting late." He was right. The last of the autumn twilight had vanished, and night had settled firmly over the city. Or at least as much of it as was ever permitted to intrude, in a place that kept going round the clock and paid about as much attention to nightfall as it did to the circuit of Jupiter around the sun.

A blaze of lights greeted them as the squad car pulled up in front of the station house. People were hurrying in and out; the revolving doors never stopped spinning. As they approached, a siren blared, causing Cara to jump.

"Take it easy," Mark said. "It's not as bad as it looks."

Maybe he didn't think so, but she found the place chaotic. People milled around, some arguing at the top of their lungs, others simply staring off into space with an attitude of resignation. Phones rang continuously, typewriters hammered away, and heavy metal doors clanged shut with a boom.

"The holding pen," Mark explained when she looked in the direction of that sound. "We're in here."

He showed her into a small room that seemed a blessed oasis of quiet in the midst of the din. The moment the door was shut behind them, she slipped into one of the molded plastic chairs and sighed. "Would you believe I've never been in a police station before?"

"Doesn't surprise me," he told her, resting one of his feet on a chair and putting an elbow on his knee. He patted his sweatshirt absently.

"What are you looking for?" she asked him.

"How's that? Oh..." He caught himself and flushed slightly. "I gave up smoking four years ago, but I still forget every once in a while."

"Is that when you took up jogging?"

He nodded. "It was that or go nuts. The tension was getting to me."

"What kind of police work do you do?" She was genuinely interested, but she also realized that she needed to talk to keep her thoughts at bay. While it was true, as she had told him, that she felt fine, she wasn't eager to dwell on the incident in the park.

He was tempted to tell her all kinds of work, because in essence a cop was never off duty. Certainly he hadn't planned to be punching out a couple of would-be rapists when he started on his evening run. "This and that," he settled on finally. "I'm in plain-clothes."

"You don't...uh...specialize?"

"Well, as a matter of fact..." He hesitated a moment, then decided that he was past the stage of hiding what he did for a living. "I'm with homicide."

She did not, as he had half expected, make the usual comment on how tough or how exciting it must be.

She merely nodded gravely and said, "I guess you keep pretty busy."

"There are times, but actually the homicide rate is down."

"Thanks to you, no doubt."

It took him a moment to realize that she was teasing him. When he did, he grinned. "I've solved one or two. Mostly, though, it's keeping the guns away from the potential killers that's doing it."

"Those men in the park," Cara said slowly, "I have no idea if they were armed or not."

"So?"

"So if they weren't . . . I'd feel like a fool for not having fought them even harder."

He looked at her closely, wondering exactly how much he should say and decided to go for broke. "A man doesn't need a weapon in order to overcome a woman. Both of those guys have plenty of muscle. You were lucky to hold them off as long as you did."

"I know. . . ."

"Hey," he interjected quickly when he saw the fear flicker in her eyes, "want a soda or something?"

She shook her head. "I'd rather just get out of here."

He went to the door, opened it, and happened to spot one of the policemen who had brought in the attackers. "How 'bout we get on with this?" he called.

The officer nodded. "Be right there."

Cara took a deep breath, girding herself for what was coming, and tried not to think too much about how different it might have all turned out if Mark Sabatini hadn't come along when he did.

Chapter 2

That wasn't so bad, was it?" Mark asked. They were in a cab on their way across town to Cara's apartment. It was around two hours since they had arrived at the police station, but to her the time seemed to have flown by. Whether because the shock Mark had predicted really had set in, or because the officers who talked with her made a genuine effort to be solicitous, giving a statement hadn't turned out to be the ordeal she had feared. Still, she was glad enough that it was over.

"Everyone was very kind," she confirmed, "even if the other officers did make it clear that they agree with you about what will happen."

"They'd have been lying if they'd tried to convince you of anything else. However," he added more cheerfully, "when I told you that, I didn't know those guys already had rap sheets as long as their arms. My guess is they'll do some time for this."

"And that's enough to satisfy you?"

"What do you mean?" he asked.

"Not that I want vengeance, if that's what you're thinking. Only that . . . there ought to be a better way. Even if those two are put away for a while, there are plenty more to take their place."

"Plenty and then some," he agreed. "Sometimes parts of this city can seem like a war zone. Which," he added, "is a good reason for you not to go wandering around on your own."

"The Mayor wouldn't like to hear you say that," she pointed out with a slight smile, "not to mention the Chamber of Commerce."

"Politicians. You can keep them."

"You're not exactly an idealist, are you?" she asked.

He looked at her from under those thick, dark lashes. "Show me a cop who is, and I'll show you a rookie."

"Don't you think that's something of a shame? After all, how do you keep going at such a tough job if you don't really believe that you can make a difference?"

"Who said I didn't believe that? I make a difference all right but not because of any ideals." He closed one hand into a fist and jabbed it into the palm of his other hand. "This is what I rely on."

Her forehead furrowed. "Brute force? That's the answer?"

"No, but judicious persuasion sure is. That and the sheer strength of the law itself. It's only as good as the people enforcing it, but it's all we've got."

Cara could see his point. He was out on the street, in the middle of what was often an extremely danger-

ous confrontation between the law on one hand and
anarchy on the other. As though that weren't complicated enough, he had to respect the rights of individ-
ual citizens and uphold the image of the police in the
community. No wonder he used to smoke.

They were pulling up in front of her building, one
of the pre-World War II cooperatives that lined the
east side of the park. As the uniformed doorman
caught sight of her through the taxi's window, he
hurried forward to open the door.

"Nice place," Mark murmured as he brushed the
man aside and helped her out himself. He glanced up
at the imposing edifice of the building and carefully
hid his feelings. This was hardly the first time he'd
been to such a place—homicides happened even to the
wealthy—but it was the first time he'd been confronted by the fact that a woman he was very attracted to lived in a world vastly removed from his
own.

"Thank you, again," Cara was saying. She presumed he wanted to get on his way and didn't feel right
about detaining him. He probably had to be up at
some ungodly hour to get to work.

"I'll see you upstairs," he said firmly.

"That isn't—" She broke off, realizing that she
wasn't eager for him to leave. Besides the fact that she
was feeling a bit shaky, he was far and away the most
interesting man she'd met in a very long time. Different, for sure, but definitely appealing.

"Perhaps you'd like a drink," she suggested as they
walked through the marble-and-gilt lobby toward the
elevators.

"That would be nice." He wondered if she had any
beer, but immediately dismissed the possibility as un-

likely. White wine, maybe, and for sure some of that fancy water that sold for two bucks a bottle in restaurants. Since he'd started jogging, he'd been meaning to try some. Four years, and he still hadn't.

The elevator was large, paneled in mahogany, and absolutely silent. It carried them to the twenty-third floor in seconds. They stepped out into a carpeted hallway, the walls of which were lined with attractive paintings in gilded frames.

"Nice," Mark murmured again, mentally contrasting his present surroundings with the way his own building had looked before it underwent gentrification. His was a whole lot better now, but nothing to compare with what he was looking at.

"I inherited the apartment," Cara said as she put the key in the lock. She hadn't meant to say that; it had slipped out unbidden. The suggestion that she was somehow embarrassed by her wealth took her aback. It wasn't true. She was using it much too well to feel self-conscious about what had, after all, been an unlooked-for windfall.

As she opened the door, she reached inside to flip off the switch that controlled the burglar alarm. She still wasn't completely used to it and had inadvertently set it off twice. The entry hall gave way to a spacious living room where floor-to-ceiling windows looked out over Central Park. Off to one side was a kitchen any number of professional chefs would have given a great deal to possess. Behind the kitchen were servant's quarters, which Cara was presently using for storage. On the other side of the living room was a separate dining area, and beyond that was the bedroom suite she occupied, which had a dressing room and a palatial bath. The entire apartment had been recently redecorated and reflected her own taste for a light and uncluttered look.

It was a taste Mark happened to share. He looked around and nodded appreciatively. "Are those windows on the alarm?"

Whatever she'd expected him to say, it wasn't that. She shook her head. "Uh...no...I didn't think it was necessary."

"Because you're twenty-three stories up? But only one floor from the roof. It'd be pretty easy for anyone to rappel down."

"Do burglars actually do that?" she asked, unable to hide her shock.

"Sure, if they think the pickings are rich enough. But, hey, I didn't mean to scare you. Just give it some thought when you're over this."

"I suppose I should...." She stared at the windows, seeing them for the first time in an entirely different light. It occurred to her that he must see the whole world that way. "About that drink..."

"Coffee would be fine."

"Are you sure? I've got some cold beer."

"Oh, well...in that case." He figured it would be some fancy foreign stuff, but in fact it was American and, more unexpected still, in a can. She didn't even seem surprised when he told her he didn't need a glass. Instead, she just popped the top on a can of soda and joined him.

When she noted the direction of his gaze, she tilted the can and laughed. "I've been trying to give this stuff up, but so far I haven't had much luck."

"It seems pretty harmless to me. Why do you want to give it up?"

"Because..." How to explain to him that the soda invariably reminded her of hot Texas afternoons on the porch of the run-down boardinghouse where she had lived with her mother, rocking back and forth on the swing and wondering if the welfare check would stretch to cover another day. Back then an ice-cold can of soda plucked from the refrigerator in the grocery store had been about the biggest luxury she'd known.

"It's fattening," she said finally.

He shrugged. "You don't look as though you have to worry about your weight."

Did that mean he thought she was too skinny? She balanced the can between the palms of her hands and wondered what to say. It had been a long time since she'd felt tongue-tied in the presence of a man. He wasn't even that good-looking when you came right down to it. A little too rough around the edges and without the social polish she had become accustomed to.

"Did you grow up in New York?" she asked suddenly, unsure how she had arrived at that question but wanting to know nonetheless.

He nodded. "In Brooklyn. Ever been there?"

Strange that he should ask, since it was directly across the river and very much a part of the city. Stranger still that she should have to say no.

"Uh...not actually. I haven't lived here long."

"Oh, yeah?"

"About two years."

"Where were you before that?"

"Texas originally, then I worked in California for a while."

"What brought you east?" he asked.

"My...father died. He left me...certain responsibilities."

Mark glanced around again at the room that looked as though it would fit perfectly into the pages of a glossy magazine. "Did he leave you the money, too?"

Cara flushed. She had already accepted the fact that he was blunt, but she hadn't expected him to be quite that direct. Her chin rose defensively. "Yes, he did."

"Old money, I'll bet."

"What makes you say that?" she asked, genuinely puzzled.

"You've got a certain...aura about you, like you were born to live this way."

Despite herself, she laughed. "Thanks, I think, but the fact is I'm not exactly a stranger to the other side of the tracks."

"Don't take this the wrong way, but I find that hard to believe."

"Why?" she asked.

"You're too refined and elegant to have ever been really up against it in life."

Weren't detectives supposed to be good judges of character? Mark couldn't have been more wrong about her if he'd tried. The little *Mona Lisa* smile that played across her mouth puzzled him. He'd said something that amused her, but he'd be damned if he could figure out what.

"That's me," she said, "refined. Care for another beer?"

He shook his head. "I didn't mean to stay this long. You need to get to bed." He meant that perfectly innocently, but no sooner were the words out than they both flushed and looked away from each other.

Cara stood, collected his empty can and her own, and carried both to the sink. As she did so, she winced.

He was at her side instantly. "Something wrong?"

"No," she assured him quickly. "I guess I'm just not as resilient as I thought I was."

"You'd feel better if you took a hot bath."

"I'm awfully tired." It was true, she was suddenly exhausted and felt as though even the effort to keep her eyes open was too much for her. Yet the idea of a lovely hot soak was all but irresistible.

Her quandary must have shown, for he said, "Look, I can hang around, if you like. Just to make sure you don't fall asleep in the tub or anything." In case she got the wrong impression, he added, "There's a basketball game on I wanted to watch anyway. You've got a TV, haven't you?"

"Yes, but..."

"On the level, I'm not trying to pull anything."

"I know you aren't," she said softly, meaning it. There was something about him—a sense of integrity, perhaps—that made her absolutely certain she was safe with him. That was not to say the faintly scary tension which exists between a man and a woman who are interested in each other was missing. On the contrary, she was becoming more vividly aware of it by the moment.

"You really wouldn't mind staying?"

"Just forget I'm here, unless you need something, of course."

That was patently impossible, but she pretended to accept it. "The television is in the armoire in the living room. There's more beer, if you'd like, and I've got a nice selection of junk food."

He grinned down at her with a light in his ebony eyes that made her heart turn over. "I figured you for the yogurt and lettuce leaf type."

"Spare me. I harbor a long-established addiction to potato chips and make yearly resolutions about giving up jalapeno dip."

"You've got that?"

"It's a sure bet."

Moments later he was happily ensconced in front of the television—she had even persuaded him to put his feet up on the polished oak coffee table—and she was running a hot tub. While it filled, she undressed, noting as she did so that she was even more bruised than she had thought. She shivered and averted her eyes from the mirror, not wanting to see the evidence of how close she had come to disaster.

The tub was—as the advertising brochure had said—big enough to hold three comfortably. Why anyone would want to, she figured was their own business. At any rate, it was also extremely comfortable for one.

A long sigh of pure relief escaped her as she lowered herself into the steaming water scented with her favorite jasmine oil. She lay back against the padded rim, closed her eyes and let the jets of water wash over her. After a few minutes, she could feel the tension draining out of her.

Drowsily, she opened her eyes and looked around the room she privately thought of as her greatest self-indulgence. It had a deliberately old-fashioned, almost Victorian, air. The tub was surrounded on all sides by panels of golden oak which matched the enclosures for the other fixtures. The walls were papered with her favorite Laura Ashley print, tiny blue and red flowers on a soft beige background. She had used the same print for the curtains and picked up the colors in the rug that covered most of the floor. A ceiling fan with an etched-glass globe at its center doubled as a light.

There were baskets of fragrant soaps and potpourri scattered around the room, stacks of magazines and plenty of luxuriously thick towels. There were times when it occurred to her that she had a bathroom bigger and certainly far more comfortable than any bedroom she had occupied before coming to New York. Move in a refrigerator and a coffee maker, and she figured she could live in it.

Certainly the tub was comfortable enough for sleeping, which was what she was very much tempted to do. Her eyelids were growing heavier by the moment. The room was growing fuzzy as she continued to stare at it through the mist rising off the bath water. She told herself she'd get out in a moment, but before she could do so, the trauma she had endured caught up with her, and consciousness slipped away.

Through a haze of fragmented dreams, she was distantly aware of a hammering sound and someone calling her name. She struggled to open her eyes, but her lids felt weighted down, as if by lead. An alarm flashed in her mind, warning her that something was wrong, but lethargy kept her from responding.

Outside the bathroom door, Mark hesitated before deciding that he'd waited as long as he could. It was more than half an hour since she'd left him in the living room. As he'd become aware of the absence of any sounds from the farther reaches of the apartment, he'd become concerned. His original intention had been merely to tap on the door, hear from her that she was okay, and go back to watching the game, which happened to be tied and in overtime. But when she didn't answer, he decided he had to do more.

The bathroom door was not the usual pressed wood, hollow variety he was accustomed to. It was made of oak and was solid all the way through. When he pressed against it the first time, it didn't even budge. He leaned his shoulder into it more firmly and was rewarded by a slight movement. With a grim look, he stepped back, took a deep breath, and went at the door for real.

The only problem was it hadn't been locked, only stuck. It flew open, and he suddenly flew into the bathroom, all but doing a triple gainer into the tub itself. Coming up just short of it, he stared down at the vision that greeted his eyes.

Good Lord, but she was beautiful. He'd known that all along, of course, but knowing and seeing were two different things. Floating there in the scented water, with her golden hair spread out around her, she looked like something Botticelli might have painted. He'd always been partial to the Renaissance artists, liking the way they handled light and managed to make ordinary things look special. Though no one could possibly call Cara ordinary. She was the stuff of fantasies, and he was suddenly having more than his fair share of them.

"I'm sorry," he murmured when it finally occurred to him that she might be a little upset about his bursting in on her.

She looked at him vaguely through heavy, languorous eyes. Only then did he realize how totally out of it she was. "I think you've had enough," he said with a slight smile as he plucked a towel off a heated rack and dropped it open. "Up and at 'em."

"Mmm," she murmured, returning his smile. Something wasn't quite right about all this, she knew that, but just then she couldn't quite put her finger on what it might be. Anyway, he was so nice and she was so tired....

Mark got the message and laughed softly. He bent down beside the tub and, not without a bit of trepidation, slid an arm around her. Her skin was so soft and silky that, for a moment, he had to stop and take a deep, restraining breath. Go easy, his better self told him. She's had one unfortunate experience today; she doesn't need another.

Not that he came even close to classing himself with those creeps in the park. He'd been raised to revere women. Perhaps that idea wasn't too fashionable these days, but let someone else explain that to his mother. She had always figured a pedestal was a pretty good place to be—in between raising six kids and helping to run the family business, of course.

Why he was thinking of his mother as he gently slid Cara out of the tub, he could only guess. Probably just to make absolutely sure he kept remembering that he was a gentleman. That was easier said than done when she snuggled against him and drifted right back to sleep.

Good for her, but he had a very clear idea that it would be some time before he managed to follow suit. His firm mouth was set in a self-mocking line as he carried her, wrapped in the towel, into the bedroom and laid her down on the bed. The room was exactly what he would have expected: large, beautifully furnished and very feminine. The bed was brass, the sheets were silk, and the prospect of sainthood was less attractive by the moment.

With a muttered curse, he realized that he could hardly leave her there on top of the covers. He managed with some difficulty to get them down without lifting her again, but not until she was safely covered did he breathe a sigh of relief. She murmured something in her sleep and smiled.

It was the smile that almost undid him. He could withstand the temptation of high, full breasts, a tiny waist, luxuriously curved hips and long, tapered legs. But that seductive little lift of her gorgeous mouth was the last straw. Telling himself that he would feel like a heel afterward but that he didn't care, he bent his head and touched his mouth lightly to hers.

She tasted of honey with a hint of spice, which he didn't even try to figure out. Her lips were warm, smooth and yielding. They parted under the slightest pressure of his. The temptation to go further was proving all but irresistible. Before the last of his self-control crumbled, he pulled back. Hastily, he tucked the covers in around her and, ignoring the soft murmur of disappointment she gave, hurried from the room.

At the door, he turned and looked back at her. She lay on her side with a hand under her cheek, the picture of innocence and vulnerability. A part of him was very definite about not wanting to leave. He ignored it and shut the door firmly.

Moving quickly, before his better self deserted him, he went back to the living room and flicked off the television. In the kitchen he found a notepad and jotted down his name and phone number, with a request that she call him if she had any more trouble. He didn't let himself think about the fact that she might choose to call for another reason.

Out in the fancy hallway, he reached back inside to reset the burglar alarm, then closed the front door and made sure it was secure. Then he beat a hasty retreat in the elevator. The doorman gave him a once-over as he stepped onto the street, but Mark ignored him. He was too busy thinking about what he had just walked away from and what the odds were that he would ever see her again.

Chapter 3

How was your weekend?" Diana Baldwin asked the following Monday as Cara walked into the offices of the Herrington Foundation on Central Park South. New York had woken up to leaden skies, heavy rain and the definite impression that winter wasn't far off.

Cara grimaced as she shook out her umbrella and put it in the stand next to the door. "Okay, I guess. I almost got mugged." She had decided that was the best way to explain the bruises visible on her wrists and throat. Though what had actually happened was far more serious, she couldn't bring herself to go into it. Especially not since she knew that while her colleagues would certainly sympathize, there would also be a certain resignation in their response. They were all tried-and-true city dwellers who had long ago accepted the fact that anything could go wrong and usually did.

"Mugged?" Diana repeated, and her soft brown eyes widened. She was from Georgia originally, looked like a slightly more ample version of Diahann Carroll, and had enough common sense to get her through several lifetimes. "Oh, honey, that sounds bad. Are you sure you ought to be here today?"

Cara smiled, slipped off her raincoat and hung it in the closet. She took a quick glance at herself in the nearby mirror, deciding that she looked a bit washed out. "I'd rather be here than at home thinking about what almost happened."

"You said that before. Does it mean they didn't get anything?"

"Nothing except arrested."

Diana's normally serene face split in an ear-to-ear grin. "You mean they got caught? Why, honey, that's fantastic! It isn't too often that somebody wins against those guys."

"I haven't won exactly," Cara said. "There's no guarantee they'll go to jail for this. But on the other hand," she added more cheerfully, "I did get off pretty lightly."

Her friend's smile faded as Cara walked over to her desk. Diana took note of the bruises. "Looks like it wasn't exactly a fair fight," she said, standing and heading for the coffee machine. "You sit down while I get you a cup. There's nothing here that can't wait a little while."

"What about that request from the crisis hot line?" Cara asked as she slid into her chair. She was still feeling rather shaky, though it had less to do with the attack on her than with memories of Mark Sabatini. Had she really, as she seemed to remember, fallen asleep in the bathtub and required his assistance getting to bed? She certainly didn't want to think so, but her mind told her differently.

She was trying to convince herself that policemen were a lot like doctors, and there wasn't any reason to be embarrassed in front of one when Diana put a steaming mug in front of her. Cara cupped her hands around it gratefully. "Thanks. I left the apartment so fast this morning I didn't stop for breakfast."

"The hot line needs more money," Diana said as she returned to her own desk. "Same as always. They'd like a meeting with you later today."

Cara sighed and reached out a hand to flip through her calendar. Like the offices themselves, there was nothing fancy about it. The smallest possible fraction of the Herrington Foundation's budget went for overhead. Diana and the two other employees earned good salaries, but other than that, expenses were kept to a minimum, which was why the offices were so simple. Of course, it didn't do any harm that Cara happened to own the building where they were housed.

"I can fit them in at 2:00 p.m.," she said. "'Country Visits for City Kids' has the morning and the drug rehab center gets the rest of the afternoon."

"You don't think you're stretching yourself a little thin?" Diana asked. She hadn't worked for Cara very long before she discovered that she preferred frank talk to any amount of beating around the bush.

"Probably," she said with a wry smile, "but what's the alternative?"

"Hire more help? It wouldn't hurt for you to give yourself a break now and again."

"I'd rather spend the money on one of our programs. We're still turning down four out of every five requests for help that we receive. More than a few of those are perfectly valid and worthy of a positive response. Unfortunately, even as well capitalized as we are, we can't afford to do everything I'd like.''

"You're still doing a whole lot more than just about any other rich person I'd care to mention. Why, just this morning I was reading on the subway coming to work about that girl, Swoozie Carter, and this party she threw for three thousand of her closest friends. Now I ask you, how could anyone even know that many people, let alone think they were friends?''

"Maybe she's just a real popular lady," Cara suggested with a grin. "Besides, don't believe everything you read. I'll bet she paid for hardly any of it.''

"How's that?" Diana asked.

"Simple. Clothing designers, caterers, wine importers, limousine companies, all sorts of outfits will provide freebies for a party like that in order to get the publicity. They write it off to marketing, and good ol' Swoozie has herself a fine time in the process.''

"I like that," Diana said, her expression making it clear that she did anything but. "Maybe next time I'm having half a dozen of my closest friends over to play bridge, I'll call up some of those companies and see if they want to chip in.''

Cara laughed and reached for the stack of mail in her in-tray. "Don't hold your breath. You know that those who need don't get, while those who have plenty have to beat it off with a stick.''

"Isn't that the truth," Diana murmured as she got down to work.

The women worked together in companionable silence for about an hour. The foundation's two other employees, both male, arrived shortly before nine o'clock. They were properly commiserative after

Diana insisted on telling them about what had happened to Cara, then they, too, went about their duties.

At ten o'clock, Cara went off to the meeting with the vacation people. It was across town, and she opted for a taxi because of the rain. The driver dropped her at the curb in front of her destination, then peeled away so abruptly that a shower of muddy rainwater drenched her coat. She shook it off as she rode up in the elevator, convinced that the day could only get better.

It didn't. The vacation program that sent poor kids out of the city for a couple of weeks each summer was in bad financial trouble. Contributions had fallen off, and government subsidies were approaching zero.

"We simply have to have more money from you," the middle-aged woman who ran the program explained to Cara. "Our other sources have been tapped to the limit, and we run the risk of disappointing several thousand children next year unless something happens to change that."

Cara nodded, knowing that the woman was giving her the unvarnished truth. "I'll see what I can do," she said, not promising anything, but knowing that she would make the utmost effort to come through for them. Children were always a top priority with her.

But so were adults who happened to be in trouble, which was why she was one of the major sponsors of the crisis hot line. Meeting with two of their representatives over lunch at a fast-food place, she listened as one of the men described their situation.

"We started out taking maybe a hundred calls a night," he said. "We're up to three hundred now and if our projections hold, we could hit double that in another year."

"What's causing the increase?" Cara asked as she took the pickles off her hamburger and put them on the side of her plate.

"The word's out that we actually help," the other man replied. Like his colleague, he was young, good-looking in a tired sort of way, and badly overworked. Both were married and had children. Cara happened to know that neither got to see much of his family these days. She hoped their wives understood.

"We're getting a lot of calls from kids," the first man said. His name was Dave Haley. He'd graduated summa cum laude from Princeton, and he could have been pulling down six figures a year at any investment firm in the country. Instead he was working eighteen hours a day, trying to help people who might as well have grown up on another planet, so different were their lives from his.

Because of his background, Cara had been a little suspicious of him at first. She'd had a hard time believing that he was really serious about what he did, which was funny, because Dave had later confessed to the same feelings about her. He'd presumed that anyone so rich, even by his affluent standards, couldn't really care about those less fortunate. Cara had briefly considered enlightening him about her own background, but she'd decided against it. That was simply something she didn't talk about with anyone.

"I'll come up with the money," she said as they were leaving the fast-food place. "It may take me a few weeks, but you'll have it."

"Thanks, Cara," Dave's friend, Philip Bradley, said. He was another tall, serious-looking WASP whom it had taken Cara some time to get used to. But in Philip's case at least there was a readily understandable explanation for his involvement with the crisis center: he'd had a younger sister who died from a drug overdose when her family failed to realize what was happening and help her.

Cara suspected that somewhere deep inside, beneath the urbane exterior, Philip was trying to work off a heavy load of misplaced guilt. He hadn't been able to save his sister, but he could and did help a lot of other kids.

"Don't mention it," she said with a smile and a wave as she left them. The rain had stopped, and she decided to walk to her next meeting. She had some time, and it would do her good to clear her mind. Even on such a busy day, Mark Sabatini had never been far from her thoughts.

As she walked, she thought back over everything that had happened between them. It was probably normal for a woman to be at least slightly infatuated with a man who had saved her as Mark had. There must be something buried deep within the female psyche that responded to such male strength and protectiveness. It would be a little strange if she hadn't kept thinking about him.

Except that when she did, it wasn't the incident in the park that she kept remembering. It was afterward, when they had shared a drink in her apartment, and she had felt both relaxed and excited at the same time. That was a pretty rare combination, and it alerted her to the fact that her feelings for Mark Sabatini weren't going to be easy to explain away, no matter how hard she tried.

Then there was the little matter of the incident in the bathroom. Why hadn't she felt at least slightly embarrassed, not to mention threatened, by having a man she barely knew see her naked? Instead, when she looked back on it, she thought the incident had been rather sweetly funny. She must have looked quite a sight floating there in the tub, all bleary-eyed and basically incoherent.

She only hoped he realized that she hadn't been faking. The previous few days had been at least as hectic as the one she was presently slogging her way through. On top of that, she'd been sleeping poorly for a variety of reasons she didn't care to examine too closely. The upshot was that she'd been pooped when she walked into the park. By the time she got into the tub some hours later, she'd been off in what an acquaintance of hers so aptly called "la-la land."

In the final analysis, what difference did it make if he thought she'd been faking or not? Despite the fact that he'd left his phone number, it wasn't likely that she'd see him again. She'd have to get a whole lot more liberated than she was before she could call up a man for a date.

But that begged the question of what she'd do if he called her. "I'll think about that tomorrow at Tara," she murmured under her breath, causing a bag lady to glance up from her sidewalk perch and give her a very dubious look.

At the moment dubious described Mark's expression as well. He was seated behind his desk at police headquarters' homicide division, his feet up on the cracked and peeling surface, his arms folded behind his head and the look in his eyes anything but encouraging.

"What do you mean, Adler, a daylong conference to 'interface' with other law enforcement personnel?"

"It seems self-explanatory to me," the nervous-looking man in front of him said. He was a civilian, a political appointee and in charge of what was dubiously called "internal communications and relations." The title always made Mark think he had something to do with solving family squabbles.

Actually, that would have been a useful function in a department known to have occasional differences of opinion within the ranks. But instead, Adler seemed intent on keeping them from doing their assigned jobs, preferably by making them attend what Mark considered useless conferences, notable only for the time-wasting quality of their presentations and the inedible quality of the long lunches they always included.

"The symposium," Adler went on, "is bringing together law enforcement specialists from the five boroughs to discuss areas of mutual concern in an atmosphere conducive to shirt-sleeve decision-making. You'll take some real, concrete results away with you, believe me."

"What I believe," Mark said, swinging his feet off the desk, "is that I'm up to my eyeballs in unsolved cases and unfinished reports. I don't have time to waste on any airhead 'interfacing.' Get my meaning?"

Adler drew himself up to his full five-and-a-half feet and affected a disappointed scowl. "The Commissioner won't like this."

"The Commissioner likes results, and right now he's got more than a few community boards breathing down his neck about those unsolved killings. Just in case you didn't see it, yesterday's *Post* went so far as to suggest that we might be trying to cover up some kind of serial murderer who's loose in our fair city."

The smaller man blanched but held his ground. "That's exactly the kind of communication failure we're working so hard to prevent. One of the major topics of the conference will be more effective commingling with the media which—"

"Commingling," Mark interrupted. "Hell, Adler, I'm interested in avoiding the more inane reporters we've got around here, not dating them."

"That isn't what it means, as you know perfectly well. If you would only make the effort to improve your communications skills—"

"I communicate just fine, especially when I'm left alone to do the job I was hired to do. Now, if you wouldn't mind bothering someone else, I'd like to finish up these reports and go 'commingle' with a couple of suspects in the Chinese restaurant killings."

"I'll have to mention your refusal to the Mayor," Adler said as he turned to go.

"Do that, and tell him we're looking for a breakthrough on the Urban Bank shooting any day now. That'll mean a whole lot more to him in an election year than a hundred conferences."

Adler took himself off in a huff, leaving a feeling of discontent behind him. The reports Mark had mentioned really did need to be done, but he couldn't seem to bestir himself in their direction. Instead, he put his feet back up on the desk and looked out the grimy window in the direction of the river. Before he knew quite what he was doing, he was deep in thought about Cara.

Had he been an idiot to leave her the night before? He could have sacked out in the living room on the excuse that he hadn't felt right about leaving her alone. That would have been the truth. He'd regretted not staying even before he'd gotten back to his own apartment, and for reasons that went beyond the urgings of his libido. She brought out a streak of tenderness in him that didn't see the light of day all that often.

He was still sitting there thinking about her when his phone rang. His brother was on the other end; in the background Mark could hear the roar of trucks and the rumble of slightly irate voices. Pauli was the foreman for a wholesale fruit and vegetable distributor. He worked at the produce market at Hunt's Point in Brooklyn, a huge, sprawling complex that served the entire city. There was less than a year's difference in their ages, with Mark being the elder. They had been close as children and had remained so into adulthood.

"I did a deal for two tickets to the Knicks' game next week," Pauli said without preamble. "Want to go?"

"Sure," Mark said, "if nothing's breaking here. How are Marie and the kids?"

"Jimmy's got strep throat again. Looks like we're going to have to have his tonsils yanked."

Jimmy was Mark's five-year-old nephew and godson, and there wasn't a whole lot Mark wouldn't do for him. "How does Marie feel about that?"

"She's scared. Me, too. But the doctor says it has to be done, so what can you do?"

"You're going to get a second opinion, right?"

"Hey, give me a break, of course I am. The kid will have the best care. Count on it."

"Sorry," Mark said, knowing that the last thing his brother needed was him breathing down his neck. "It's just you know how I feel about the kid. If he needs anything... or if the bills look bad..."

"We can handle it," Pauli assured him, "but thanks. How about coming over this weekend and spending some time with him?"

"Any way I can, I'll be there."

"Good. Hey, you haven't forgotten about Mom and Dad next month?"

"Of course I forgot. It's only their fortieth anniversary. What's the big deal?"

"Smart guy. Davey thinks he's found the stereo we want to give them. It's got everything, including a state-of-the-art CD player. A friend of his, in the business, recommended it and is giving him a price."

Mark grinned, glad that Pauli couldn't see his expression. Everything his family ever bought was on a deal, for a price, had some kind of break attached to it. Not that any of the Sabatinis were hurting for money; they weren't rich, but they worked hard and did all right. It was just that walking into a store and paying full price for something went against the grain.

"I probably won't get a chance to take a look at it," he said, "so you see what you think and if it looks okay, just tell me my share."

"It better be okay," Pauli said. "Davey swears there's nothing fishy about this one."

Davey was their youngest brother, at twenty-eight still the baby in the family. He had, on one or two occasions, been known to get in over his head and need rescuing by his brothers. But his heart was in the right place.

"He's a good kid," Mark said. "I'm willing to bet he's come through."

They talked a few minutes longer before Mark hung up and reached for the jacket slung over the back of his chair. Automatically he checked the pistol in his shoulder holster and patted his inside jacket pocket to be sure his badge was there. He'd been checking the same things for so long that the motions barely registered. His mind was firmly on the case he was going to investigate as he left the office and headed for his car.

Chapter 4

A week later, Mark called Cara. He'd been thinking about her steadily, particularly at night when he lay awake, staring up at the ceiling and wondering why he couldn't sleep. It wasn't much of a mystery. A certain cool, elegant, surprisingly down-to-earth blonde had him tied up in knots. Simple solution: date her, sleep with her, get her out of his system.

He laughed at the thought. He'd never had much success as a macho user of women, who had a brief shallow relationship and then was on to the next quarry. Long before the sexual revolution crashed down around everyone's head and made monogamy fashionable again, he'd been extremely selective in his relationships. As a result, they'd been few and far between, but at least he could look back on a life that left him with nothing to be ashamed of.

Still, it bothered him that he wasn't married. He looked at Pauli with his loving wife and three kids, and at his sisters, two of whom had taken the plunge, and he couldn't help but envy them. Sure, it wasn't always easy for them, but he thought their lives were a lot more worthwhile than his own.

What it came down to was that he was ready for a woman he could get extremely serious about, not somebody who came from such a different world from his own that there didn't seem to be any possibility of a shared future.

All of which hardly explained why he couldn't stop thinking about Cara. He finally gave up trying to analyze his feelings and picked up the phone.

She answered on the third ring, sounding a little breathless. When she heard his voice, she was silent for what seemed to him like a very long moment. Finally, she said, "It's nice to hear from you."

"I was wondering how you're doing." Also what it would be like to go to bed with you and wake up there the next day, to sit around and talk, share confidences, find out what makes you laugh or cry. None of which he said. Out on the street, he took calculated risks. When it came to his heart, he felt too vulnerable.

"I'm fine," she said. "I heard from the arresting officers. It seems you were right on both counts."

"How's that?" He hardly remembered what he'd told her, so taken up had he been in simply being with her.

"You mentioned the chance of a plea bargain, but you thought that with their records they might have to do some time after all."

"How did it work out?"

"They pleaded guilty to a second-degree felony charge and got three years each. The policeman said they'd probably be out in a year, but he seemed to feel it was a victory to get them behind bars for even that short a time.''

"He's right. We won this one.''

"I guess so. All I'm really interested in is putting the whole experience behind me.''

Did that mean him, too? The idea that she might not want to see him again made his stomach tighten. He had enough confidence in himself to have not seriously considered that possibility before now.

"I'm glad you're okay,'' he said. "You've been on my mind a lot.''

Silence again, and then Cara said, "I've been thinking about you a great deal, too.''

He expelled a silent sigh of relief. She didn't play games. Add honest to what was already an impressive list of qualities. "How about dinner one night soon?''

"That would be nice.''

"Friday okay for you?''

"It should be. What time would you like to pick me up?''

At seven o'clock that Friday evening, Mark was standing in front of Cara's building looking up at the elaborate stone masonry over the entrance. It was a lovely night, a little warm for autumn, with a clear sky in which a few stars shone despite the bright city lights. He was dressed in a pair of gray slacks, a navy blazer and a button-down blue shirt that he'd picked up on sale at Brooks Brothers. He liked their clothes, even if his family did kid him about them. Maybe there was some truth to the idea that they were as much a uniform as what he'd worn on patrol, but they suited him all the same.

There was a different doorman on duty. Despite the clothes, he didn't look any too enthusiastic about Mark. He laughed to himself, thinking that east-side doormen probably had some kind of radar for picking out working stiffs like himself. It made him feel good when Cara was buzzed and she said over the intercom, "Please send him right up."

The elevator and hall were exactly as he remembered them. Not only did he fail to hear sounds coming from the doors he passed, but he didn't smell anything either. Put him in ninety-nine percent of the apartment houses in the city and he'd have at least some idea of where he was from the smells. His own small building near Columbus carried a permanent fragrance of coffee beans, basil, lemon oil, and the Giorgio perfume that no fewer than three of his female neighbors, and one of the males, favored.

But on Cara's turf there were no smells at all. Either they weren't allowed or rich people smelled of something he couldn't even pick up on. Sort of like dogs being able to respond to whistles in a frequency humans couldn't hear.

He straightened his blue and red striped tie, and told himself to stop being so hung up on her money. They were going out to dinner, they'd have a good time, and then they'd see. No sweat.

At least not until she answered the door, at which point he forgot all about his good resolutions and simply stared. She looked . . . he couldn't think of the word, wasn't sure there even was one. Suffice it to say that at that moment all other women went completely and permanently out of his mind.

"Is something wrong?" Cara asked, looking up at him. He was frowning at her, which didn't do her nerves any good. She'd been anxious all day, trying to figure out what to wear and how to act. He hadn't said where they were going, so she'd dressed fairly casually in a beige silk shirt and a pleated skirt over which she could throw a matching jacket.

Her hair was swept up into a loose chignon, she wore simple gold earrings and her makeup was so discreetly done as to be all but imperceptible. After a brief tussle with herself, she'd left several buttons open on her blouse so that there was the briefest glimpse of the cleft between her breasts. Underneath the blouse she wore a bra of almost sheer lace and silk. Although she didn't realize it, her nipples were slightly visible through the fragile material.

"Wrong?" Mark repeated. He shook his head. "Not that I can see. You look . . . uh . . . great."

Some of her concern faded. She smiled and stood aside to let him in. "So do you. Brooks Brothers?"

"What did I do—put the labels on the wrong way?"

"No, but there's a certain look that comes from that place. It suits you."

He was pleased, but didn't want to make a big thing of it so he just followed her into the living room. There had been a few changes, he noticed. "You had the windows wired."

She looked mildly chagrined. "The man from the alarm company assured me that the sensors were all but invisible."

"They are, except to someone in my line of work, or to a would-be crook. It's good you had it done."

Despite herself, she warmed to his praise, discovering in the process something she had already suspected: she liked pleasing him. Before she could take that thought any further, she asked, "Would you care for a drink?"

"How's your beer supply?"

"Restocked and with a couple on ice."

She walked over to a trolley set with crystal stemware and a silver ice bucket out of which several cans of his favorite all-American brew peeped incongruously. Mark shook his head and laughed. "There aren't too many people who would think of doing that. How did you know beer always tastes better when it's iced down?"

"Any girl who grew up in Texas knows that."

He accepted the can she handed him, wondering if he ought to break down and use a glass since they were in the living room. But she didn't seem to think it was necessary so he let it go. Cara poured herself a very dry sherry over ice with a chunk of lime. They sat down next to each other on the couch.

"I've never been to that part of the country," Mark said as he crossed one long leg over the other. "Course, I've watched *Dallas* a few times."

Cara laughed, took a sip of her drink and regarded him over the edge of the glass. "Texans don't think that's much of a reflection of their lives. In fact, they tend to make fun of it."

"You mean you don't all live on big ranches and fight over oil wells?"

"Oh, of course we do, but we dress better and have bigger jewels."

He grinned, not sure she was kidding. Maybe compared to her life, the show was small potatoes. "Do you miss it?" he asked after he had taken a swallow of his beer.

Rather to his surprise, she shook her head firmly. "No, I was glad to leave Texas and I've got no plans for going back."

"Why? What's wrong with the place?"

"Nothing. There's a part of me that still believes it's the center of the world. But...there are reasons why it's better for me to be here."

He wanted to ask her what those were, but it was getting late. They had a reservation at a restaurant popular enough to give away tables when patrons were tardy. His would be saved, but Mark didn't feel right about that.

"We'd better get a move on," he said, standing up. "This place where we're going, Rudolfo's, tends to get a crowd these days."

Cara shot him a quick, startled look. "I've read about it, but I haven't been there yet." She was no stranger to "in" restaurants, at least not lately, but Rudolfo's was one that had so far escaped her. Its reputation, however, had not. She caught herself wondering how a policeman, even a detective, could possibly afford it.

"Do you...uh...eat here often?" she asked as they were walking down the two steps that led to the restaurant's entrance. It was only a few blocks from her apartment so they'd strolled over.

"Once or twice a month," Mark said. He held open the door, stood aside for her, and nodded to the hatcheck girl. "How's it going, Lena?"

The girl was a redhead, tall, good-looking and poured into a simple black dress, its elegance failing to disguise her flamboyant figure. She looked at Mark appreciatively and cast Cara a speculative glance. "Not bad. Staying out of trouble these days?"

He held his hand out flat and tipped it from side to side. "Now and then. Rudy working tonight?"

The girl nodded. "I'll tell him you're here."

The maître d' had joined them. He gave Mark a broad smile, which extended to Cara, and showed them to a table in a secluded alcove off the main room. It had been set for four, but the other two place settings were whipped away as they took their seats.

Cara sat down, looked at Mark over the crystal and fresh flowers, and said, "Either they are paying detectives a whole lot more than I thought, or there's a story here."

He grinned, shot the cuffs of his shirt, and obliged her. "A couple of years ago my cousin Rudy came to me and said he was tired of working for guys who don't know anything about running a restaurant in this town. He wanted to go into business for himself. I happened to have something put aside, so I gave it to him. He called it a loan; I told him not to make a big deal out of it. Two years later, I found myself owning half of the hottest restaurant in New York." He shrugged lightly. "I figure I should actually have maybe a quarter of the place, but Rudy's being stubborn. We'll work it out. In the meantime I get a lot of good food."

That was certainly the truth, if the meal they proceeded to enjoy was anything to go by. After a mussel soup flavored with hot red pepper and served with slices of whole wheat Italian bread, they moved on to fillets of red snapper simmered in wine and flavored with anchovy and parsley. With it came a bottle of Fiano di Avellino chilled to precisely the right temperature.

The service was swift and discreet, so much so that Cara was hardly aware of dishes being removed and glasses being replenished. Mark's cousin Rudy dropped by their table briefly. He proved to be a pleasant, if serious, man in his early forties who evinced a genuine affection for Mark and seemed pleased to see him with Cara.

Over a dessert of *zuccotto*, the traditional Florentine dessert of nuts, pound cake, liqueurs and chocolate, they continued to talk about life in New York, what they did and did not like about it, other places they'd been and what they'd thought of them. But over the espresso, Mark turned the conversation in her direction.

"You never did tell me," he said as he leaned back in his chair, looking replete and relaxed, "why you prefer New York to Texas."

She fiddled with the stem of her glass and hesitated before answering. "I didn't exactly say that. It's just that I left some bad memories in Texas and I'd prefer not to relive them by going back."

His dark brows drew together. "Bad how?"

Her gaze moved past his shoulder, and she shrugged. "My parents were divorced; I lived with my mother. It's an old story, the kind a lot of people can tell. There's no point in making a big production of it."

"If you don't want to tell me about yourself, you don't have to."

"It isn't that...."

"Hey, it's okay. We just met each other. Maybe you think I wouldn't understand."

She looked at him directly then, seeing the gentleness behind what was a rather formidable visage. He was a very strong man, both inside and outside, but that didn't mean he couldn't be tender. She had already experienced that aspect of his nature once, and had to admit, if only to herself, that she wouldn't mind doing so again.

"On the contrary," she said softly, "I have the feeling you'd understand completely. But it's very hard for me to talk about it."

He held her eyes, looking deep into them, as he slowly nodded. "There's no rush."

Simple words, but they gave her a welcome sense of stability. With a minimum of fuss, he'd let her know that he wanted to see her again, but that he wasn't going to push her into anything she wasn't ready for. That was quite a change from the men she usually met, who all too often seemed to think they should be rounding home plate before they'd even come up to bat.

Mark's cousin saw them out. He took Cara's hand, held it between both of his own and gave her a meaningful look as he said, "I hope we'll be seeing you again."

Outside on the sidewalk, Mark tilted back his head and laughed. "Maybe I should have told you that my family isn't really big on subtlety."

"I thought it was very sweet," she said, biting her inside cheek to keep from laughing with him. "He's a very nice man. Besides, he really cares about you. You should be glad."

"I am," he said more soberly. "It baffles me how people can get along without families to care about them and drive them crazy. Must get pretty lonely."

"It does," Cara said quietly.

"Hey, I didn't mean..."

"I know you didn't," she said as she put her hand lightly on his arm. "But you're right, people who belong to closely knit families are very fortunate."

"Don't you have any relatives at all?" he asked as they started walking in the direction of her apartment. He had covered her hand with his own and could feel the fragile delicacy of her bones. A brief image of her nude in the tub flashed through his mind. He fought it down resolutely.

"I suppose I must," she said, "though not on my father's side. Any relatives he had would have come forward when he died."

"Because of the money?"

She nodded. "It draws flies like something I won't mention."

"That's an interesting way to put it. It almost sounds as though you don't like being rich."

"Actually, I don't think of myself that way. Really, I mean it," she added when he shot her a skeptical look. "I realize that I live in a very nice place, wear nice clothes and so on, but I have the feeling that you think my life is very different from the way it really is."

"How so?"

"Well, for one thing, I don't go to places like Rudolfo's a couple of times a month."

"Touché," he said with a laugh. "Okay, how else is it different?"

Instead of answering directly, she posed a question. "Do you realize that with all the talking we did this evening, you never asked me what kind of work I do?"

He looked at her, startled. "I just assumed..."

"That I don't work at all? Well, you happen to be wrong. I run the Herrington Foundation and no, that doesn't mean I spend my days having lunch and planning charity balls. It's a bit more basic than that.''

He had stopped in the middle of the sidewalk and was staring at her. ''You're the outfit that helps support the Police Athletic League. I didn't put it together until now, but the name's the same.''

''That's us,'' she said. ''We help support about two dozen organizations of which the PAL happens to be one. They do a good job. I'm glad we can help.''

''It sounds as though I have some heavy-duty reassessing to do. I really did think you were just a happy-go-lucky rich girl. Not,'' he added quickly, ''that I've got anything against those.''

The corners of her mouth turned up in what he already recognized as a signal that her sense of humor was piqued. ''For one thing,'' she said, ''they make great bookends. Put them down somewhere with their nails wet or a face pack on, and they won't go anywhere until you come back and rescue them.''

''You...uh...don't have a whole lot of affection for your particular socioeconomic group, do you?''

''I would probably put it a bit more directly than that, but you've got the general idea. There are some nice people who happen to have money, just as there are nice people who are poor. But generally, in my experience, wealth doesn't bring out the best in human nature.''

''It doesn't seem to have done you any harm,'' he pointed out.

''Thanks, but I came to it late in life.''

''How late?''

''About a year ago.''

''Oh...part of those Texas memories?''

She nodded. ''The end of them.''

"Still don't want to talk about it?"

The prospect was tempting, but she wasn't quite ready. "Maybe soon," she said, and thought that for the first time, the prospect of reliving her past didn't seem quite so frightening.

Chapter 5

When they got back to her apartment, she invited him in. The question of whether or not to do so had been on her mind since before he'd arrived to pick her up. She wasn't one to rush into anything, and she didn't intend to start now. But the thought of the evening ending, as it inevitably had to, left her feeling vaguely sad. She wanted to delay dealing with that as long as she could.

"Would you like some coffee?" she asked as she unlocked the apartment door.

They'd both had two cups at the restaurant; the chances that he wanted more were remote, as they both knew. But he nodded anyway. "That would be fine."

"I've got some decaffeinated somewhere," she said as she rummaged around in the kitchen cabinets. It occurred to him that she lived in a place where there were meant to be servants. The lack of them must have something to do with her former life.

"I've been meaning to switch over to that," he said, "but I still drink the regular stuff."

"Good," she said with relief. "So do I, which means I know where it is."

As she ground the beans, he sat down at the polished oak table and watched her. She moved gracefully, without any self-consciousness. The kitchen was large, and she had to walk back and forth across it several times. He liked watching the way her skirt swung around her slender legs and her breasts moved slightly.

"Thanks," he said when she set the cup in front of him. She'd noticed that he took it black and didn't bother asking him about milk or sugar.

"I had a good time this evening," she said as she sat down opposite him. "You're nice to be with."

Her frankness took him aback slightly, but he decided very quickly that he liked it. "I feel the same way, and I'd like to see you again."

"Are you . . . ?"

"Involved with anyone else? No. How about you?"

She shook her head. "I haven't been in a long time."

He gave her a very direct look. "Don't expect me to say I'm sorry."

She laughed and drank some of her coffee. There was a clock on the kitchen wall, a pretty thing with flowered tiles on its base. It was getting on to one in the morning.

"I'm on duty tomorrow," he said.

"Saturday?"

"It happens. We've got a couple of cases we can't break. Every day that passes makes it less likely that we will, so we have to keep pushing."

"I see . . . it must be rough sometimes."

He finished his coffee and rose to go. She stood also and came around the table to him. They were standing very close together. He reached out a hand and let his fingers curl around her chin. "It's hard on the families, especially the spouses."

She understood what he was telling her; if they did get involved, she should expect to have to make some concessions, probably big ones. "Do you get shot at often?" she asked him, only half-facetiously.

He chose to answer her seriously. "I've been fired at maybe a dozen times in fifteen years. That's actually quite a lot, but it's because of the particular kind of cases I handle. I've been wounded once, in the left arm."

She nodded, struggling to take in what he was telling her. This was a man who stood on the line between stability and violence. In a very real sense, he was a soldier and, like all soldiers in war, a target.

"What about the other way around?" she asked, hearing the note of breathlessness in her voice. She wasn't excited; on the contrary, she felt deadly calm. She had to be to deal with the situation.

"You mean have I ever shot anyone?" She nodded. "Once, a guy who came at my partner and me with an automatic rifle."

"What happened?"

He frowned slightly as though the outcome was self-evident. "I killed him. It went up before the review board, and I was cleared."

"That's all there was to it?"

"No," he said slowly. "I still think about it from time to time, trying to see if there was anything else I could have done. He was nineteen years old."

"You saved your partner and yourself."

"There is that."

But it still bothered him that he'd killed someone. She sensed that he'd never be able to merely slough it off, which told her a lot about the kind of man he was.

So did the way he bent his head and gently took her mouth with his. The kiss was a tasting, a savoring of her and of them both. He parted her lips slowly with the tip of his tongue and traced the ridge of her teeth before plunging more deeply. His arms tightened around her, and she was pressed against a rock-hard chest completely lacking the layer of fat most urban men possessed. Whether by virtue of his profession or from simple inclination, Mark kept himself stripped down to the essentials. He was in good shape and he intended to stay that way. What he didn't know and couldn't have guessed was the effect it had on her.

She felt at once infinitely protected and oddly threatened. He was gentle, so she felt safe. But he was also very strong and was becoming aroused. She was over her experience in the park, and there was nothing in her background to make her afraid of sex. But she was suddenly, almost overwhelmingly afraid of him.

Then she realized that she'd mistaken the source of her fear. He might be the innocent catalyst that brought it out, but what really scared her was the intensity of her own feelings. She wanted him as she had never wanted any man before. There was actually no comparison between anything she had experienced in the past and what she was going through right then.

Whatever she thought she'd known about desire had just been exploded out of existence by the sheer force of the passion he unleashed in her.

It was a very scary prospect for a woman who prided herself on her self-control.

"I think," she said shakily when at last they drew apart, "that you'd better go."

He hesitated, wanting to disagree but knowing that she was right. He wasn't about to push her. Especially not now, when he knew what was possible between them. "All right," he said. "I'll call you in the next few days."

"I could call you instead."

He looked at her directly. "I'd like that."

They left it there. Mark went home and, to his surprise, slept well. He woke six hours later feeling refreshed. As he shaved and showered, he caught himself whistling. That made him laugh and he was still smiling when he slipped on his jacket, checked his holster, and went out to face the world.

Cara didn't sleep quite so peacefully; she woke several times during the night from dreams which must have been very pleasant because she wanted to slip back into them. Despite her interrupted rest, she awakened early. On the weekends, she generally liked to sleep in a little, but she had barely opened her eyes before she realized that closing them again would be pointless. A deep current of excitement running through her precluded the possibility of further rest.

As she dressed, she gave some thought to what she might do that day. She had a list of errands that needed to be run, but after that she would be free. Had Mark not mentioned that he'd be working, she would have been tempted to call him then and there. They could have seen a movie or just gone for a walk. A glance out the window showed her that the day looked warm and pleasant, probably one of the last of its kind they would have before winter arrived.

Wearing pale blue jeans she'd had for more years than she could remember and a soft plaid shirt, she tossed a sweater around her shoulders, grabbed her purse, and left the apartment. Her first stop was the post office where she picked up stamps, next was the dry cleaner to discuss how a silk blouse that had been pale pink had ended up bright red. After listening to promises of reparation, she went on to the grocery store.

Most New Yorkers shopped in supermarkets, like people just about everywhere else. But in very affluent neighborhoods such as Cara's, the specialty grocery store remained an institution. Somewhere she had read that only the rich could afford to maintain the traditions of yesteryear, and she had to agree there was something to that. "Mallone's Irish Grocer," as the place was billed, was a relic of an age when cooks and serving girls with the soft, lilting accents of the old country had ventured out each day to shop for their wealthy employers.

It still retained an air of quaintness and dignity, despite all the changes of recent decades. Now the servants who shopped there tended to be Hispanic or black, though the occasional Irish nanny still wandered in with her well-chaperoned charges. There was also a handful of neighborhood residents like Cara who had the money to be waited on hand and foot, but who preferred to look after themselves, even when that meant lining up at the butcher counter to see what the pork chops looked like.

"They're a bit small, Mr. Mallone," Cara said with
a smile. "I think I'll take two."

"Right you are, Miss," the burly man on the other
side of the counter said. Whether or not his name was
actually Mallone was a matter for conjecture, but
everyone called him that and he didn't seem to mind.
He and his wife—his "Mizzus," as he referred to
her—owned the store. Three teenage boys, including
one of their sons, helped out.

"We've got a nice bit of veal today," Mr. Mallone
said as he wrapped up her purchase in brown paper
and tied it with a length of string. Cara had often
wondered whether he continued to use so archaic a
packaging method simply because he had always done
so and hadn't thought of changing, or if it was a carefully considered part of the store's overall ambience.
Every time she saw Mr. Mallone driving to work in his
Cadillac, she suspected the latter. Not that she
minded; she liked people who paid attention to detail
and she found some humor in the fact that he was
earning a considerable income from the yearnings of
people like herself for a simpler way of life.

"How about a few chicken breasts, instead," she
said, "skinned, if you would."

While he saw to that, she glanced around the store.
"Mizzus" was at her usual post, perched on a stool
behind the cash register. Cara didn't think she had ever
seen the plump, gray-haired woman stray from that
position. Her son, Charles—never Charlie—was busy
shelving boxes of soap powder. One of the boys, Raymond, came in from making a delivery. He smiled at
her shyly, and she smiled back.

"Will there be anything else, Miss?" Mr. Mallone asked, handing her the chicken breasts, which were also neatly wrapped in paper and string.

"Not today, thanks."

He wished her a good day, and she headed for the front of the store. Along the way she picked up a couple of tomatoes—ridiculously expensive but vine-ripened in a greenhouse and therefore vastly better than the usual cotton wool imitations. She selected a handful of fresh basil to go with them.

"Mizzus" rang up her purchases, took her money, and gave her a disapproving glance. "You ought to be bundled up better, Miss Herrington, if you don't mind my saying so. You're asking for a nasty cold in that flimsy shirt with just a sweater tied around your shoulders."

"It's nice and warm today, Mrs. Mallone," Cara said.

The older woman sniffed. "Pneumonia weather, it's called, and right that is. People go around dressed like it's still summer, and next thing they know they're sick as dogs."

Cara murmured something more or less appropriate and took her leave. She had seen Mrs. Mallone two or three times a week for the past year, and the woman had yet to say anything remotely cheerful to her. She was one of those people who could suck all the light and energy out of wherever they happened to be. Cara felt sorry for her, but had no trouble dismissing her from her mind as she started off down the street at a jaunty pace.

After she had returned to her apartment and put her purchases away, she sat down at the kitchen table with a glass of orange juice and leafed through the paper.

Bloomingdales was having a sale. She toyed with the idea of walking over, but hadn't yet made up her mind when the phone rang.

It was Philip Bradley calling about the crisis center. "I'm sorry to bother you on a weekend," he said, "but things are going from bad to worse here, and I wondered if you've made any decision about the funding?"

Cara restrained a sigh. She would have liked nothing better than to throw him bundles of money and tell him to do whatever he liked with it. But the realities of the foundation's financial resources, versus the demand on them, made that impossible.

"I've been giving it a great deal of thought," she said, "and I'm definitely interested in increasing our level of support. But before I do that, I feel I need a better understanding of what's going on there and of where funds could best be used."

"I'll be glad to give you any information I possibly can," Philip said. In the background, she heard a young child squealing. He was calling from home, stealing time from the few precious hours he had with his family.

"Information isn't going to resolve my questions," she said, "at least not the kind someone else can give me. What I'd really like to do is work at the center for a while. Do you think that could be arranged?" She'd done that sort of thing before and had found that it worked out well. Immersing herself in the day-to-day running of such an operation not only helped her to understand its financial needs, but also ensured that the foundation didn't contribute to inefficient, poorly managed organizations. She didn't think the crisis center fell into that category, but she had to be sure before increasing support.

"Of course it can be," Philip said enthusiastically. From his tone, she had to conclude that he was completely behind the idea. "You can start whenever you like. In fact—"

"Let me guess," Cara said with a laugh. "You're shorthanded because it's Saturday and for the same reason you're expecting a busy night, so you'd like me to start this evening."

"I'm sure you have plans...."

"Actually, I don't." He could make of that whatever he liked. So long as the only man she'd been interested in in ages wasn't available, she felt no qualms about being dateless on a Saturday night. "What time should I plan to start?" she asked.

He told her, and said he'd be sure to have someone on hand to brief her properly before she began. "The night shift runs from 8:00 p.m. to 4:00 a.m.," he told her. "It'd be a good idea to try to get some sleep before you come down."

Naps had never agreed with her, but she did lie down that afternoon and finally managed to doze off listening to the sounds of traffic far below her windows. She woke up a couple of hours later feeling musty-headed and took a shower before fixing herself a light meal.

The crisis center was housed in a ramshackle building far downtown that also contained a purse factory and two button manufacturers. A creaking freight elevator let her out on the third floor, where a fresh-faced young man greeted her.

"Hi," he said, sticking out his hand. "I'm Zack. Phil asked me to show you the ropes."

The elevator opened onto a large room about thirty by thirty feet, which was furnished with a dozen desks, each with a plain, black telephone. The people behind the desks ran the gamut from those in their early twenties to senior citizens. They all looked serious, attentive and committed.

Zack showed her to a gunmetal gray table that looked as though it might have seen service on a torpedoed battleship long ago, and then been salvaged from the ocean. Cara tried to make herself comfortable in the rickety folding chair he offered. As she did so, she glanced around. The peeling walls were covered with notices about various aid projects, community meetings, commission hearings and the like. There was a large handwritten sign that read: "Man is immortal, not because he alone among creatures has an inexhaustible voice, but because he has a soul, a spirit capable of compassion and sacrifice and endurance."

"Interesting," Cara said, gesturing to the sign. "Who said it?"

"William Faulkner, in his speech accepting the Nobel prize for literature."

"Didn't he also say something about Keats's 'Ode on a Grecian Urn' being worth any number of little old ladies?"

Zack laughed and nodded his head. "Yeah, he was trying to make the point that good writing is worth any sacrifice, including personal relationships."

"Seems a bit contradictory to me, talking about compassion, but putting down little old ladies."

The young man shrugged. "Geniuses are always contradictory. So are nuts and sometimes it's hard to tell the difference."

"I suppose you get plenty of nuts here," Cara said.

"This city breeds crazies the same way it breeds cockroaches," Zack agreed, "but mostly what we get are lonely, frightened, desperate people who just need to reach out to someone. Actually, the fact that they pick up the phone and call us is a sign that they're not completely gone. We never hear from the really lost ones."

Cara took a deep breath. She had the definite feeling that she was in for a rough night. "What happens if I slip up and say the wrong thing?"

"You get struck by lightning, of course, what did you think?"

She laughed, a bit nervously, but she'd gotten the point. She was human, like the other workers and like the people who would be on the other end of the phone. She'd do her best; no one could ask for more than that.

Chapter 6

By the time Cara got home shortly after dawn the next day, she felt as though she had gone another couple of rounds with the creeps in the park. She ached deep in her bones, her head throbbed, and she had the disconcerting sense of having been away far longer than she actually had been. Perhaps because she had been in a world so vastly different from her own, where the landscape was barren of everything except hope. At least, as Zack had said, the people who called still had that; if they hadn't, they wouldn't have bothered to pick up the phone.

During her hours at the crisis center, she had given out information about drug and alcohol abuse programs, explained to a woman how she could get job retraining, helped a man figure out how to deal with his rebellious adolescent son, and simply listened as innumerable people poured out their troubles to her.

If there had been nothing else to it, the experience would have been unbearable; no amount of dedication could bring a person back to go through it again and again. But right along with all the problems and troubles, she had caught a strong sense of simple human strength and determination to hold on against all odds.

It made her realize that while she could sympathize with the people who called, she felt no temptation to pity them. They were admirable in their willingness to reach out and ask for help, possibly the most courageous act a person could undertake.

Philip had come by in the middle of the night while she was on the phone. Her immediate thought, when she caught sight of him getting off the freight elevator, was that he was trying a little too hard to impress her. But then she realized from the way the other workers merely glanced up at him that his presence at such an hour wasn't unusual. In between taking calls, she had talked to him while he perched on the corner of her desk and sipped hot, black coffee.

"Zack says you're a natural," he told her.

She laughed and shook her head. "I don't think so, but I certainly am learning a lot."

"Any chance that you might stay with us for a while?"

She thought about that. Her days were very full as it was, and she was hoping that Mark would be taking up her evenings, if not her nights. Yet she had to admit that what Philip was suggesting had some merit.

"It's a possibility," she said at length. "I should at least be able to help out a few times a week."

"That would be great," he assured her. "We don't encourage people to work more than that because there's a strong danger of burnout."

Crawling into bed as the sky turned light, she knew what he meant. Voices, phrases, brief glimpses of other people's lives careened through her mind. She tossed and turned in her sleep, and wasn't at all displeased when the ringing phone woke her up.

Groggy as she was, her first thought as she reached for it was that perhaps Mark was calling. The disappointment she felt when she heard a voice other than his brought her abruptly upright.

"Hope I haven't caught you at a bad time," Tom Skinner said. He was a securities specialist she had been introduced to several weeks before at a fundraiser. About thirty-five, divorced, Ivy League background, six-figure annual income, he had all the attributes of the successful New York bachelor. He also happened to be a nice man.

"No," she assured him, "I was just catching up on some rest, but if I'd slept much longer, I'd have a problem tonight. How have you been?"

They exchanged the usual pleasantries before he asked if she was free for dinner that Friday night. Cara hesitated. She and Mark had been out exactly once, and she had no idea when she would be seeing him again. She also had no reason to think that he wouldn't be dating other women despite the fact that he wasn't seriously involved with anyone. Therefore, she had every reason to go out with Tom.

Except that she didn't want to. It was nothing personal; if he'd called a few days before, she would have agreed without hesitation. But in the meantime, Mark had happened, and that changed everything.

"Look," she said, "I have to be honest with you. I've met someone who seems to be one of those cases of instant attraction. I expect I'll be seeing him again and it may develop into something serious. So I don't think I should be going out with another man at the same time."

"I see...." Tom thought for a moment, then chuckled wryly. "You know, when we were introduced and talked briefly, one of the things I really liked about you was that you were very straightforward. I see so much deviousness in my line of work that it's really refreshing to find someone who's not into that."

"Thanks," she said as she sat up straighter against the pillows and brushed the hair out of her eyes with her hand. "But there are times when I think I could benefit from a little subterfuge."

"Maybe, but I've got the feeling that if this guy you've met is what you seem to think he is, he'll appreciate you exactly the way you are."

It was difficult to know what to say to that. Tom was being very understanding, which she appreciated, but he was also virtually a stranger, and she didn't feel comfortable discussing such personal feelings with him.

Being a nice man, and genuinely perceptive, he understood that, too. They talked a little while longer about general things before she hung up and sat staring at the phone for a moment. Without letting herself think about it too much, she picked up the receiver again and punched in Mark's number.

* * *

"I hope you realize," she said a few hours later when he picked her up, "that it's a very big deal for a girl from the Texas boonies to call a man for a date."

"I kind of figured that," he said with a grin. He wasn't as elegantly dressed as he had been the night before, but neither was he wearing his sloppy jogging outfit. The jeans he had on were clean and well pressed. With them he wore a beige turtleneck sweater that made his broad chest look even bigger and emphasized the swarthiness of his coloring.

"What tipped you off?" she asked after they had left her apartment and were walking up Fifth Avenue in the direction of the Metropolitan Museum of Art. There was an exhibit of Chinese jade she had been meaning to take in, and when he had asked her what she wanted to do, it had popped into her mind. Now she was wondering if he was going to be bored.

"You sounded a little breathless," he said cheerfully. "Like you couldn't quite get the words out."

"I was that bad?"

"Don't worry about it," he said, taking her hand as they walked along. "It's kind of nice to have the shoe on the other foot."

"What do you mean?"

"Every time a man calls a woman up for a date, he's nervous. You put yourself on the line, risk rejection, all that sort of thing. If she says no, you're left wondering what you did wrong."

Cara thought of Tom and was doubly glad that she'd explained her situation honestly. "I never thought of it that way," she admitted. "Most men have come across as pretty self-assured to me."

"Actors, all of us. Inside we're a mass of quivering jelly."

She cast him a blatantly skeptical look from under her long lashes. "Are you describing yourself?"

"Absolutely."

"Forgive me, but I don't believe you. I'm not sure I've ever met anyone more self-confident."

It was his turn to look at her sidelong. "You really think so?"

She nodded firmly. "You know who you are and you're content with that. I'm not saying there's nothing in your life you wouldn't change, but you like yourself and that counts enormously."

What could he say? She was right. "Wouldn't you say that describes you, too?" he asked.

She thought about it for a moment, then nodded. "Yes, it does. I've recently gone through an enormous change in my life, but it hasn't made me a different person. In a lot of ways, I'm the same woman I was back in Texas."

"Which you still haven't told me much about."

"Here's the museum."

He held back slightly, standing on the sidewalk in front of the high marble steps. "Not yet?"

She met his eyes, seeing again the tenderness she had sensed before. With some embarrassment, she said, "It's nothing dramatic. Don't think that or when I tell you, you'll wonder what all the fuss was about."

He shrugged, and they started up the steps together. "It's the day-to-day living that makes a person, not the high or low points. That's what makes real life different from fiction."

"I saw an interesting quote from William Faulkner yesterday," she said as they entered the main lobby and paid admission. "He was talking about what makes the human spirit immortal."

Mark rolled his eyes. "Don't tell me you curl up with one of his books for fun."

"Lord, no. I make great resolutions to read serious stuff and still end up with armloads of romances."

"My sisters read those; they love them. But where does Faulkner fit in?"

Cara took a catalog off a nearby table and began flipping through it. "I was working at a crisis center yesterday. The quote was in a sign on the wall."

"Do you do that regularly?"

She shook her head. "It was my first time. We help to fund them, and they've asked for an increase in support, so I'm taking a closer look to find out how it could best be used."

They had entered the room where the jade exhibit was taking place. Display cabinets held glistening treasures in a broad range of colors beginning with the shades of deep green most commonly associated with the mineral but also including delicate hues of pink and white.

"Isn't that incredible?" Cara said softly as she stood staring at a foot-high statue of a woman. The precision of the carving was such that she expected the tiny figure to move at any moment.

"Late Qing dynasty," Mark said without reference to the small, typewritten card below the statue. "Probably a concubine at the royal court."

Cara turned to him, making no attempt to hide her surprise. "How on earth did you know that?" A quick glance at the card had confirmed that he was right.

He shrugged and looked slightly embarrassed. "I majored in Oriental religions in college. Jade is a symbol of spiritual forces, of the world beyond this one. Works done in it frequently have a religious significance, though not in this particular case." He looked again at the little statue.

"I should have guessed," Cara teased. "There's a direct connection between the study of Oriental religions and police work."

"Actually, there is," Mark said, "or at least I've been able to use a lot of what I learned about tolerance and patience. At any rate, while it wasn't the most practical education, I don't regret it."

"Where did you go to school?" Cara asked as they moved on to the next display case.

"CUNY," he said, giving the abbreviation for the City University of New York. "It was free back then."

"Must have been tough to get into, in that case."

"You had to be pretty sharp," he admitted.

"Did you study any Chinese?"

"As a matter of fact, I did. That almost finished me off. Nice Italian boys aren't meant to speak Chinese."

Cara laughed, thinking that he was nice, but he was hardly a boy. From the moment he had appeared at her door that day, she had been vividly aware of him as every inch a man. Moreover, she sensed that the same awareness of her as a woman was running through him. It was leading them to an inevitable destination, which she found herself looking forward to more and more.

"Do you remember any of it?" she asked.

"Enough to make some of the folks in Chinatown laugh pretty hard. They don't quite know what to make of it when I open my mouth and come out with some of their lingo."

"It must help if you're trying to get them to loosen up and tell you something."

It did, to the tune of enabling him to crack the Chinatown restaurant murders earlier that day. News of the arrests would be on the television that night and in the papers the following morning. She'd be bound to see it, but he didn't see any reason to bring it up.

"How about getting a bite to eat?" he asked a while later as they were leaving the museum.

"Sounds good to me."

They strolled through the park, coming out on Central Park West. Mark was pleased to see that she showed no hesitation about walking near where the attack had happened, but he couldn't resist asking her if she had been in the park alone since then.

Cara shook her head. "I still walk home from the office, but not that way."

He didn't mistake the note of regret in her voice. "I know it's tough, but you must realize it's for the best. Why would you want to push your luck?"

"I don't, but there must be thousands of people who walk through the park every day without anything bad happening to them."

"Sure," he agreed, "and there's nothing to say that you couldn't do it every day for years and never have another bit of trouble. On the other hand . . ."

"Why take the risk?"

"You've got it."

"I can't play it safe all the time," she protested.

He stopped, put a hand on her shoulder and turned her to him. "I didn't say you should do that," he said, and right there in the middle of the street with traffic whizzing by and people hurrying about their business, he kissed her very thoroughly.

"You do that awfully well," Cara said a few moments later when she had recovered enough breath to speak.

"You're no slouch yourself." They were walking again, hand in hand, their strides matching as though they had been doing so for years.

Cara hesitated, then decided it was better to speak up now than regret it later. "I haven't had all that much experience."

"I didn't think you had."

She shot him a surprised glance. "But you said..."

His hand tightened on hers. "A woman or a man can kiss well and do everything else without having been to bed with a lot of people. It's the feeling that counts, not the expertise."

"I agree, but that's a very unusual attitude."

It clearly didn't bother him to be out of step with what the majority of people might think. He was a man who charted his own course and stuck to it. They had that in common; she'd never been one to live by the standards of others.

At a small café off Columbus Avenue, they ate sandwiches washed down by espresso and talked about books they'd read. Mark read mainly nonfiction, especially history. Cara preferred novels; besides romances, she liked mysteries and the occasional big, different book that came along and made everyone sit up and take notice.

"I loved the novel I just finished," she said. "It made me feel as though I was actually living back in the Neolithic era."

Mark agreed with her. "The thing that struck me, though," he said, "was that we don't seem to have changed all that much."

"Is that a hint of cynicism I hear?"

He shrugged. "Maybe. Police work can certainly make you that way. But there really seems to be something called human nature that's followed us straight from the cave days."

"It's not all bad either," she said. "That's when people first began to have a sense of loyalty to family and clan, and when they learned how to cooperate, to work together for the greater good."

"They learned a few other things, too."

"Such as?"

"Men and women started looking at each other as individuals and began forming attachments that went beyond sexual desire."

She sat back in her chair and met his gaze directly. His eyes, shielded by slightly lowered lids, were even darker than usual, yet she could feel the fire darting from them. It seemed to reach out and touch her as a lover would. Her awareness of the restaurant faded. She lost all sense of the bustling waiters, the other patrons, the myriad sights, sounds and smells that made up her surroundings. There was only Mark, holding her with his eyes, caressing her. All else was shadow without substance.

Chapter 7

They saw each other twice more in the following week, both times for dinner. On Saturday they went down to Chinatown and stuffed themselves on Szechuan food, then took in a movie about the Vietnam war. It proved tough to sit through, but well worth the effort. They emerged from it silent and thoughtful, their minds full of painful images of the war.

"I was only a kid when that was going on," Cara said as they walked back toward where Mark had parked his car. "I didn't think I remembered much about it, but that movie brought a lot back."

"In spades," Mark murmured. He was holding her hand, and she could feel that his palm was slightly damp despite the cool night. Throughout the movie she had been aware of him becoming tenser by the moment, his attention riveted on the screen except when he seemed compelled to tear it away briefly, as though to catch his breath.

Quietly, she asked, "How long were you over there?"

He shot her a quick glance. "What makes you think I was?"

"The way you've been the last couple of hours, the way you are now. Either you were there yourself or someone you cared about a great deal was killed there."

He was silent for several minutes as they continued to walk down the street. When they paused to wait for a traffic light to change, he sighed and said, "Both. I did one tour, twelve months. Five days before we were due to go home, my best friend—a guy from my old neighborhood who I'd grown up with—was killed. I spent my last few hours in 'Nam identifying his body."

"You know I'm not going to say anything stupid like how sad or that must have been tough. But I would like to know how you managed to put that behind you and get on with your life, as you've obviously done."

"I had a lot of help," he told her frankly. "Mostly from my family. My father was in World War II, but he didn't make the mistake some older guys did of thinking 'Nam was like that. He knew without anyone having to tell him that there was a big difference. When I got home, he sat me down and made me talk even though that was the last thing I wanted to do. He dragged it all out of me, everything I'd seen and done. Then he gave me some good advice."

"Which was?"

"Go to church, thank God for giving me my life, and then get busy putting it to the best possible use."

"And that worked?" It seemed so simple that she couldn't imagine how it could have, yet there was no denying that Mark was a whole, sound man free of the anguish that plagued some of those he'd served with.

"It took a while," he said, "and a lot of thinking, but in the end that was what it came down to. I needed to do something positive to counteract all the destruction I'd experienced."

"So you went into police work?" It was beginning to make sense now, how a man of his obvious intelligence and education had been drawn into an occupation that was not only dangerous but didn't pay especially well. He needed, above all, to make a contribution to his world, to try to leave it a better place than it had been when he arrived. She knew the feeling.

"I had an uncle who was a cop," he said with a reminiscent grin. "Uncle Louie started on the force back when Italians weren't all that common in this line of work. His partner for years was an Irish guy named Callahan. After the two of them decided that they actually weren't all that different from each other, they used to get together pretty often with their families. Aunt Lucia would bake lasagna, Mrs. Callahan would make corned beef, everybody would wind up with indigestion, and nobody cared because they all had a great time."

"That's a nice story," Cara said softly. "What happened when you told your uncle that you were thinking about joining the police?"

"He said I was out of my mind."

She shot him a quick glance to see if he was kidding, saw that he wasn't, and asked, "Why? Didn't he like the idea of a nephew following in his footsteps?"

"Are you kidding? He wanted me to go to law school and get rich. He said only suckers became cops."

"Why didn't you listen to him?"

"Because I heard what he was saying underneath the words. Uncle Louie was one of the happiest people I ever met. I don't mean that he went around laughing and grinning all the time; actually, he was a pretty serious guy. But he was satisfied deep down with himself and with what he was doing in his life. That's what I wanted, too. Besides, I knew he'd try to discourage me at first, to see if I really meant what I said."

"What did he do once he was convinced that you did?"

"He gave me all the help he possibly could, telling me what to expect at the Police Academy and later, on the street. He told me things I'm using to this day, tips that have helped keep me and other people alive."

"He must have been a terrific person," Cara said softly. "What happened to him?"

He gave her a surprised look. "Nothing, he retired a few years ago and moved to Florida. I hear from him every once in a while. He's doing fine."

"But...the way you spoke of him in the past tense...I thought..."

Mark shook his head ruefully. "I didn't realize I was doing that. It's a habit cops get into. Once a guy's left the force, it is sort of like he's died."

Cara had no response to that. He had just told her, whether he realized it or not, exactly how committed he was to his work: it was his life. She had expected that it might cause some problems for them, but she hadn't realized the potential was so great. That took her aback and caused her to reflect very carefully on where their relationship was going.

Mark felt the slight withdrawal in her and realized, belatedly, what had caused it. He waited until they were driving away from the garage where he'd been parked before he asked, "Having second thoughts?" He tried to sound casual so she wouldn't know how anxious he was inside, but his voice was huskier than usual.

"Sure," she said. "Aren't you?"

His hands tightened on the wheel. "I guess so. After all, whatever your life was like back in Texas, you're a rich girl now. You live in a world I only occasionally visit, and you've got opportunities I'll never even know about."

As she opened her mouth to protest, he went on hurriedly. "But we've also got one or two things in common, not the least of which is that we happen to be very attracted to each other."

She couldn't help but smile at him despite the slight flush warming her cheeks. "You figured that out, did you?"

He laughed, settling back in his seat, feeling more relaxed now that he knew she could kid about it. "I always was perceptive."

Cara sniffed softly. "Maybe so, but you sure don't have to be to figure out how I feel. Even if I'd wanted to, I couldn't hide it."

It was true that the last time he'd held her in his arms, when he'd picked her up that evening, he'd kissed her so long and tenderly that she had come very close to suggesting they forget about dinner. Only the most deeply rooted sense of caution had stopped her. It was still early days yet, she still didn't know him all that well, she was still trying to play it safe. But somehow she didn't think any of that was going to last much longer.

Neither did he. Quietly, he asked, "Are you busy next Saturday?"

That was a week off; he never asked her out that far in advance, not because of any lack of consideration on his part but because his schedule was too erratic to allow for it. Wondering what had changed, she shook her head. "No, I'm not."

"Good. We're having a little family get-together. I thought you might like to come."

"Oh . . . that sounds very nice."

Mark shot her a glance and burst out laughing. "You look like you just got invited to your own execution. It won't be that bad, I promise."

"I know," she agreed hastily, "it's just that I have this image of your family as . . ."

"What? Big, boisterous, nosy?"

"You got it," she admitted, "but I know I'm probably way off base."

"Dead on, actually. Sure you haven't already met them?"

"Not a chance. What will they think of me?"

"My brothers will tell me I don't deserve you. My sisters will pick up on the fact that you're a warm and giving person, and come down on your side right away. My mother will try to find out how you feel about having children, and my father will just sit back and enjoy the whole thing."

"You make it sound so simple." She was sure it would be anything but. She had no experience with close-knit, loving families and no idea of how to act when she was in the middle of one, which was where she was sure she would be. She had a quick vision of herself surrounded by a crowd of handsome, lively, sharp Sabatinis taking a very close look at what she had to offer as a potential addition to their ranks. It was anyone's guess what they would make of a slightly overwhelmed blonde who was rapidly falling head over heels in love with their son.

"It'll be fine," he told her. "They're going to be crazy about you. Just one thing..."

"What?" she demanded anxiously.

"Don't tell them Texas isn't really like *Dallas*. That'd break my mother's heart."

"I won't breathe a word," she promised. "Heck, if you think it would help, I'll get one of those dresses like the actresses on the show wear."

He shook his head. "Not a good idea. I'd like my little brother Davey to be able to go on living."

"What do you mean?"

"You could show up in sackcloth, and he'd only need one look to figure he'd died and gone to heaven."

"Does that mean he likes blondes?" she asked with a laugh.

"Blondes, brunettes, redheads, he's impartial. But you could dye your hair green, and he'd go for it. All the Sabatini men have a lot of appreciation for a beautiful woman."

Despite the small voice in the back of her mind counseling caution, she warmed to the compliment. But she still felt compelled to be honest. "I've never thought much about the way I look."

He accepted that readily enough. "I can see how you've never had to. It's just there for you."

Whether she wanted it or not. She wondered if it had ever occurred to him that beauty was a two-edged sword; it made some things easier and a lot of others harder. "When I was a kid," she said slowly, "I was too tall, too skinny and had too many freckles. I couldn't put one foot in front of the other without tripping and when the very rare boy tried talking to me, I started to stutter."

"You've changed," he pointed out laconically.

"I'm not sure it's for the better. There's something to be said for having people see you as a person, even an unattractive one, rather than as a beautiful object they'd like to possess."

"Is that how most men act around you?"

"There have been times," she said carefully, "when it's seemed that way, which is why I haven't dated much."

"Anybody who hasn't bothered to look past the outside, to the person you are, has missed a great deal."

"Thank you," she said gravely, "but it's occurred to me that you've had a similar problem."

He glanced away from the road for an instant. "How so?"

"Aside from the obvious fact that you're a very attractive man, people do tend to have preconceived notions about the police, don't they?"

He nodded even as he tried to digest the fact that she thought he was good-looking. He didn't think of himself that way. "Uh...yeah, I guess so. People have all sorts of ideas."

"I have to admit you're not what I would have expected."

"How so?"

"I'm embarrassed to admit it, but you're much more complicated than I would have figured. You're strong but gentle, perceptive but idealistic, something of a loner but also devoted to your family. That's a lot of contradictions to deal with.''

She had him down pat, which did nothing for his equilibrium. He hadn't suspected that she already understood so much about him. But when he thought about it, he realized that he was equally well-attuned to her. A very special kind of intimacy was developing between them that had nothing to do with going to bed together. Yet.

When he pulled up in front of her building, he put the car in park and turned to her. In the glow from the streetlamp, she looked very young and a little nervous. He sensed that she knew exactly what was coming.

''Are there guest spots in your garage?'' he asked.

''Yes, why?''

''Because I'd like to stay over, and if I leave my car on the street, it's going to get towed. Either that or some cop is going to spot the police I.D. on the windshield and let it go. That might seem like a little thing, but I'd rather avoid it.''

''You know,'' she said slowly, ''I'm beginning to think there's some truth to the claim that New York is different from every other place.''

''What makes you say that?''

''Because here we sit discussing what to do with your car which, I think you'll admit, is really not as important as what you said about staying over.''

He shot her a wry grin. ''I was hoping you'd sort of let that slip by.''

Holding his eyes and smiling herself, she shook her head. ''Not a chance.''

''Of staying over or slipping by?''

She hesitated a long moment before she said, "Slipping. The garage entrance is around the corner."

He was a very gentle lover at first. As they undressed together in her bedroom, his hands wandered over her with tender intensity. He was slow and deliberate in his savoring of her, as though all the time that ever had been or ever would be was theirs to enjoy. When she had dressed for their dinner date, she had put on a beige silk blouse with a row of tiny pearl buttons, pairing it with tailored black velvet slacks and a matching jacket. The jacket was dispensed with before they ever reached the bedroom, as was his own. But the blouse—with its buttons—was not so easily removed.

He smiled wryly as his fingers fumbled with the first of the slippery little pearls. "The zipper was a great advance for civilization; so was the Velcro fastener. Buttons have been obsolete since both of those came along."

She breathed in the heat and power of him as her hands ran lightly down his back, feeling his muscles tense through the fabric of his shirt. "I guess I'm just an old-fashioned girl."

"Hmm...hey, I got one." He looked so pleased that he'd managed to conquer the first of the buttons that she couldn't help but laugh.

"I hate to tell you how many more there are."

"Spare me. Anyway, anticipation is good for the soul."

"In that case," she murmured as she nuzzled his throat and the clean line of his jaw, "we're going to be in great shape, spiritually speaking."

"Fantastic," he agreed huskily, making enough headway to expose the high, full curve of her breasts peeking out above the lacy edging of her bra. His arm around her back pressed her closer as he bent his head. She felt the warm brush of his mouth on her.

A soft moan escaping from her deepened as he slid his hand past the delicate fabric and cupped her gently. "So beautiful," he murmured, his thumb rubbing back and forth over her straining nipple. She felt the motion at the core of her being, where a warm, liquid heat had begun to spread. Sweet languor swept over her, weighting her eyelids and making her knees go weak.

She was glad of his strength as she sagged against him, letting the iron hardness of his body support her. Almost without realizing it, she had opened his shirt to reveal skin glowing like honey and touched by the memory of the sun. Whorls of hair as dark as that on his head teased her fingers. She sighed with deep, feminine pleasure and rubbed against him as a seductive kitten would.

Mark prided himself on a large degree of self-control. It was absolutely essential to his line of work, but it was also a characteristic he had possessed since childhood and had come to almost take for granted. But it suddenly seemed to have deserted him. His broad chest rose and fell sharply as he fought against the impulse to toss her onto the bed and make short work of the whole business.

That was never a serious possibility. He wouldn't have behaved in such a way with any woman, but certainly not with Cara whom, he realized, he had come to care for deeply. She had to be cherished, pleasured and treated with the greatest tenderness before he gave in to his own needs.

"Oh, Lord," he whispered thickly, "I think I've got a problem."

"What's that?" she murmured, thoroughly distracted by the arrow of silky hair that pointed the way down his chest to his flat abdomen and beyond.

"My mind's saying one thing, and my body's saying another."

She lifted her head and gazed at him with slumberous eyes and lips slightly parted. "The message seems pretty clear to me."

"You don't understand." He caught her shoulders and pulled her gently upright until their eyes met. "I want this to be perfect for you."

"It will be." The simple directness of that statement pulled him up short. He needed a moment to realize that she truly believed it. Far beyond any consideration of technique, any thought of her own satisfaction, she simply wanted to belong to him.

"Cara..." he whispered her name like a prayer. Then he took a step back and, still holding her eyes, stripped off the rest of his clothes. She watched him with a tiny smile playing at the corners of her mouth and the clear, direct light of appreciation in her gaze. Their movements were orchestrated toward a single goal as she followed his lead. Denim and silk, linen and velvet fell together onto the carpeted floor.

She had left a single light burning beside the bed that cast soft shadows over them both. Cara's breath caught in her throat as she stared at him. Naked he seemed somehow larger and even more male than he had before. Along with his clothes a veneer of civilization had been removed from him. She was vividly conscious of the enormous differences between them which, for a moment, frightened her.

He saw the brief flicker of concern that darted through her eyes, and in that instant something changed within him. He had the sudden, odd sense that what had not yet even occurred between them would become one of the most treasured memories of his life, something to look back on together as the beginning of far more. It was a very risky presumption, the world being the way it was and relationships between men and women being always subject to change, yet he couldn't shake the overpowering conviction that he was about to make love to the woman with whom he would spend the rest of his life.

"What are you thinking?" Cara whispered, watching the play of emotions across his face. He had looked surprised, then pleased, then very... purposeful. No other word described the way in which he reached for her, lifted her gently into his arms and carried her to the bed.

"I'm thinking," he said as he lowered her onto the mattress and came down beside her, "that love isn't turning out to be the way I thought it would be."

"L-love?" She must have heard him wrong, which was not too surprising given the dazzling play of sensations rippling through her. The sheets were cool beneath her back, while his hand resting lightly on her breast was hot. She was caught between the two, a willing prisoner to her own desires.

"I always presumed," he said as he lay back on his side and studied her with undisguised pleasure, "that when I fell in love with a woman, it would happen slowly, almost without my being aware of it. Maybe that is how it works with some people, but I sure was wrong about myself."

"Are you telling me that you...?" She couldn't quite get the words out, so intense was the pleasure she felt as his hands wandered over her, stroking her from throat to hip.

"I love you, Cara," he said, smiling down into her eyes. "I could hold back on saying that, but it seems important to put it into words before this goes any further. Something very important is happening between us."

She agreed with all her heart and soul. Her hands trembled as she raised them and cupped his face, feeling the strength of the bones underlying his burnished skin. "You're right, Mark, it is very important. You've had a lot more experience loving than I have because of your family, but even I can recognize my feelings for what they are. I love you." The sheer, heady delight of saying those precious words made her laugh. "And it feels wonderful. I can finally understand why people get so crazy in this state."

He rolled over, drawing her with him, and tangled his fingers in her gleaming hair. His mouth teased hers, his tongue sliding gently past the ridge of her teeth to explore hers. "You're going to understand more than that," he said. "We both are."

And he proceeded to demonstrate exactly what he meant. For Cara, a new world unfolded, one inhabited by sensations she had never before experienced and delights she had never even imagined. She clung to him as he took her from height to dizzying height until they were both caught in a sensual whirl leading inexorably to a pinnacle of shattering fulfillment. At the last instant, she cried his name and dug her nails into the taut skin of his back. Everything she was or had thought she could be exploded inside her and she felt herself reborn.

Chapter 8

My folks bought their house in Park Slope thirty years ago," Mark said as they were driving across the Brooklyn Bridge on their way to the family celebration a week later. "Their friends thought they were crazy to scrimp and save the way they had to in order to afford the place. But Mom was determined and Dad went along with her, figuring she had pretty good instincts. Anyway, now they live surrounded by Yuppies and shake their heads every time somebody mentions how much their property is worth. You could offer them a million dollars, and they wouldn't sell because it's home to them, but they still get a kick out of it."

"I can imagine," Cara said. She turned away from looking out the window at what was admittedly a rather dreary day and gazed at him instead. All sense of the gray sky and the incipient threat of snow vanished. He was wearing a black turtleneck under his tweed sports jacket and a pair of black wool trousers. His thick ebony hair was neatly combed, he was freshly shaved and he looked perfectly composed. No one, looking at either of them, would have been able to guess that less than an hour before they had been locked in a passionate embrace.

The memory of what had passed between them brought a warm flush to her cheeks. He caught it out of the corner of his eye and grinned. "Too warm in here?" he teased.

She shook her head. "It's fine. Will there be many people at the party?"

"A few more than usual. Didn't I mention that it's my folks' anniversary?"

Cara swallowed hard. He had conveniently managed to forget that. "Are you sure it's a good idea for me to go? After all, I don't want to intrude...."

"I already told them you were coming."

"Oh."

He braked for traffic and shot her another glance. She saw the humor dancing in his dark eyes and decided it was singularly inappropriate. "If I show up without you, I won't get in the door."

"I find that hard to believe."

"You don't know my family. They're very excited that I'm finally bringing a woman home for them to meet. Besides, Rudy gave a very good report on you."

"Remind me to thank him," Cara murmured dryly.

"Seriously, you've got nothing to worry about. Just relax and be yourself."

Easier said than done, Cara thought. Her stomach was twisted into a knot when they left the car some five blocks from the Sabatinis' house—the nearest parking spot they could find—and walked the remaining distance. As they did so, she noticed clusters of people heading in the same direction who, upon seeing Mark, waved to them.

"A *few* more than usual?" she asked. "It looks as though most of Brooklyn is turning out for this."

"Mom thinks it's a waste to get everything ready for a party if a lot of people aren't going to come. When my sister Connie got married, they had three hundred people at the reception, which was held at home."

"How could they possibly fit that many people into their house?"

"They couldn't. It turned into a block party. Fortunately, one of the guests was the captain of their police precinct. You have to have a permit for a block party, but he took care of it after the fact."

"Is it going to be like that today?" Cara asked nervously. They were nearing the Sabatini residence, a three-story townhouse of red brick with a tiny scrap of a garden out in front. A flight of stone steps led up to the front door through which was passing a steady stream of people, all of whom seemed to know each other.

"I don't think it will get that bad," Mark said. "We tried to keep this to the immediate family and friends, so figure on seventy or eighty people."

"Oh, my God."

He laughed and put an arm around her shoulders. "They're going to love you."

That showed what he knew, Cara thought grimly. She wasn't Italian, she had what they would undoubtedly regard as a funny accent, and in all likelihood she wasn't dressed right. Fat chance they'd love her.

"Mark," a round, genial-faced man called as they climbed up the steps, "what you been being a stranger for? I haven't seen you in the store in two, three months."

"I've been busy, Uncle Dominick," Mark said as he embraced the man who was regarding Cara with unabashed interest. "You know how many bad guys there are in this town."

"Too many. You should get into a decent line of work where you don't mix with such scum. I tell that to your papa all the time. But enough. You brought such a lovely lady and you don't introduce her?"

Mark took care of the courtesies as Cara smiled cautiously. She had the very clear impression that Uncle Dominick's shrewd black eyes missed nothing, which he confirmed a moment later when he said, "A nice name, Herrington. Very... American."

"I'm from Texas originally, Mr. Sabatini," she said. Might as well get it out as fast as she could.

He nodded sagely. "Texas... big place, lots of cowboys. But call me Uncle Dominick. What are we standing around on the steps for? Come," he said as he took her arm. "Maria, Mark's mother, she'll want to meet you."

Cara cast Mark a desperate glance, but he was struggling so hard not to laugh that he was of no help. Still, he did follow along and by the time they had reached the parlor, he had deftly replaced Uncle Dominick at her side.

Despite the milling crowd, Cara could see at a glance that the house was graciously furnished and spotlessly clean. The parquet wood floors gleamed with what could only be years of polishing. They were covered by Oriental rugs of excellent quality. A crystal bowl filled with fresh flowers was set on a marble inlaid table she recognized as Victorian. The parlor was similarly furnished, with overstuffed couches and chairs and a scattering of mahogany tables. Wonderful aromas filled the air, but Cara was barely conscious of them. Her attention was focused on the tall, muscular man standing by the marble fireplace at one end of the parlor. Beside him was a slender, blond woman of undeniable beauty.

"My folks," Mark said as he led her toward them. Just then, the woman caught sight of him, and her lovely face broke into a warm smile. "Look at you," she said with a laugh. "So handsome. You make me feel like an old lady to have such a grown-up son."

"Don't be silly, Mama," he said as he embraced first her and then his father.

"Listen to the boy, Maria," the elder Sabatini said with a grin. "You could live another hundred years and still not be an old lady. Being married to me keeps you young."

"Hush, Joseph," she said with a reproving tap on her husband's broad chest. "Don't you see Mark has brought someone with him?" Her hazel eyes swept over Cara with undisguised interest, which did not lessen as Mark introduced her.

Instead, Maria merely nodded and, still looking at her, said quite seriously, "You're very beautiful, you know."

"Uh...thank you," Cara murmured. She was taken aback by the older woman's frankness and didn't know what to make of it.

"Now, Maria," Joseph said, "you'll embarrass the young lady." To Cara, he added, "Don't be concerned by my wife's frankness. She's simply wondering how long you and Mark have known each other, and whether you intend to marry. Also, how you feel about children.''

"Enough," Mark said, shaking his head wryly. "It was all I could do to convince Cara to come here in the first place. Keep on like this and you'll have her running out the door."

"Of course we won't," Maria said with a smile. "She looks far too sensible to do anything like that. Aren't you, Cara?"

"As a matter of fact, I am." The encounter, strange though it might be, was turning out better than she had thought. She felt oddly comfortable with the Sabatinis, perhaps because their directness left her with no doubt as to where she stood with them. That was a welcome change from the confusion she had known in her own family.

"Naturally," Maria went on, "Mark would bring you when we have so many people there's hardly a chance to talk, but we'll make the opportunity anyway. Meanwhile, enjoy yourselves. There's so much food I'm warning everyone they don't go home until they're stuffed."

"Don't worry, Mama," Mark said as he kissed her cheek. "We skipped breakfast."

"Did you have to say that?" Cara demanded a moment later as they left his parents and made their way toward the dining room, where an enormous buffet was set out.

"Say what?" Mark asked.

"About our skipping breakfast. What will they think?"

"That we wanted to save our appetites?"

"You know that isn't all. If we skipped breakfast, that means sometimes we have breakfast, and that means..."

He stopped, turned to her and burst out laughing. "I don't believe it. You're a prude."

Around them, several people overheard and cast interested looks in their direction. Cara turned bright red and held up a hand to hush him. "I am not," she whispered. "But I don't want your parents to think badly of me."

His laughter faded, replaced by gentle understanding. "You don't have to worry about that. They're very moral people, but they know perfectly well that we're both adults who obviously care for each other."

"They love you so much," Cara said. "Anything you did would be fine with them, but I'm a different story."

"First," he said, steering her toward the buffet table, "you're wrong; anything I did wouldn't be fine. My parents have always been very strict with their kids. That's how they managed to raise six of us and keep their sanity. Sure, they know I'm an adult now, but if I was up to something they thought was wrong, they'd still let me know.

"Second," he went on as he handed her a plate and took one for himself, "you've got it in your head that they want to find something wrong with you when the opposite is true. Have you got any idea how long they've been waiting for me to bring a woman home? Now, not only have I finally done it, but she's gorgeous, sweet, intelligent and loaded with class. Hell, if we had a fight right now, this instant, I'd bet anything they'd throw me out and keep you."

Cara didn't believe him for a second, but listening to him she did feel better. At least well enough to cast a hungry eye on the assorted dishes laid out for their enjoyment. "Good Lord," she murmured, "there's enough here to feed an army."

"Nothing would disappoint Mom more than if somebody managed to get out of here today with even a tiny bit of room left in his stomach."

"She can relax, there's no danger. What's that?" she asked, pointing to what looked like stuffed pasta rolls lightly coated with sauce.

"My mother's cannelloni. It's famous. Here, try some." He put several on her plate, which he proceeded to cover with an assortment of salads, meats, cheeses and fresh fruits. When she finally protested that she had enough, he relented, only to add, "We'll come back for the rest."

They found seats in a corner of the living room. They were near the grand piano where a young man was playing a medley of popular songs, but far enough away so that they could talk comfortably. Cara took a bite of the cannelloni and closed her eyes in ecstasy. "I'm giving up sex," she said.

"What's that?"

"You heard me. I've found something better."

"Give me that," Mark said, reaching for her plate.

She laughed and held it out of his reach. "On second thought," she said, "maybe I'll go all out and indulge in both."

His dark gaze met hers, bringing memories of the predawn hours when they had awakened together in her bed and, still half-asleep, reached for each other. The swift ripening of their intimacy astounded her. She had never felt so completely relaxed with anyone, nor so constantly excited. He made all her senses come vividly alive, so that the simplest experience took on an aura of the extraordinary.

"I'm sure if you asked her, my mother would teach you to make these," he suggested. "You could whip up a batch, we could eat them in bed, and then..."

"You're terrible," she said, giggling.

He leered at her encouragingly and was about to continue, undoubtedly in the same vein, when they were interrupted. "So, what's this I hear?" asked the smiling, dark-haired man who joined them. "Mom said to come over and meet Cara. That must be you." He held out his hand to her and as she took it, said, "I'm Pauli, Mark's younger and better-looking brother. My wife, Marie. Marie, Maria, it confuses everybody, but don't worry about it."

"How do you do?" Cara said as she took in the pair. Pauli did look a great deal like his brother, though he was somewhat shorter and broader around the waist. His reference to being better looking had clearly been ironic. His wife was a petite, smiling woman who seemed a bit tired.

Mark evidently thought so, too. He stood up, giving her his chair. "Sit down, Marie. How's Jimmy?"

"He's fine," she said softly, explaining to Cara. "My five-year-old. He has to have his tonsils out. All he understands is that he gets ice cream afterward, so he can't wait."

"Great kid," Mark said. "Wait until you meet him."

"Do you have other children?" Cara asked.

Marie nodded. "Three, two girls and another boy." She cast a fond look at her husband who stood with a hand resting gently on her shoulder. "The Sabatinis tend to have big families."

"What's big about four?" Pauli asked.

"You have the next one and find out," Marie said, laughing. She gave Cara a woman-to-woman look and asked, "Do you come from a big family yourself?"

She shook her head. "I was an only child, actually. My parents separated before I was born."

Beside her she felt Mark's start of surprise. In an unguarded instant, she had just revealed more of her past than he had been able to find out since they met. She could only wonder at the effect his family had on her, that she had felt prompted to do such a thing.

"How sad," Marie said with genuine sympathy. "It must have been hard on you growing up."

"There were problems," she admitted, though she didn't elaborate. Her natural reticence about personal matters was reasserting itself.

"Did you grow up in Texas?" Pauli asked.

Cara nodded. She realized that she couldn't refuse to answer without appearing rude. "My mother was from there originally, so it was natural for her to go back when her marriage ran into trouble."

"Is she still there?"

"No...she died several years ago." Before anyone could comment on that, she went on brightly. "This is a wonderful party. Your parents are very hospitable."

That turned the conversation toward remembrances of other family occasions. The talk flowed easily, but beneath it Cara was acutely conscious of Mark's steady scrutiny. He was clearly mulling over what he had learned about her, and she did not doubt that he would insist on knowing more. Nor could she really blame him. Given the nature—and the direction—of their relationship, he had a right.

But for the moment it was enough to simply relax and enjoy herself with his family. They made it very easy. Over the course of the next few hours, she met a dizzying assortment of aunts, uncles and cousins, all of whom seemed to know all about her. Already she was "Cara" to them which, as more than one pointed out, was an Italian name.

"Are you sure," Mark's youngest brother, Davey, asked, "that you aren't Italian originally?"

"I'm afraid not," Cara said with a smile. "I was named for a character in a novel my mother was reading when I was born."

"Oh, well, everybody can't be Italian," he consoled her. "It's all right, don't worry about it."

"Thank you," she said solemnly. It hadn't taken her very long to decide that Davey, for all his attempts at sophistication, was still very much a little boy at heart. When they met, he immediately turned on the charm and suggested that she was wasting her time with his brother. She didn't make the mistake of taking that seriously, to his evident relief.

Behind the brash exterior she glimpsed a still slightly uncertain young man of considerable potential who simply hadn't quite settled into himself yet. That he would she didn't doubt; he had the same solid core of strength and stability that seemed to characterize all the Sabatinis.

When she said as much to Mark, he looked at her gravely for a moment before he replied, "Davey's okay. I worry about him from time to time, but basically he's fine. We pretty much all know what we're looking for out of life."

"I've definitely gotten that impression," she said, thinking of the speed at which their relationship had developed. "There's only one thing that bothers me."

"What's that?"

She glanced around at the crowded room. "I don't think this is the place."

"Give me a hint."

Realizing that he wouldn't relent until she did so, she said quietly, "Just tell me one thing: if I hadn't called you after the first time, would we have gotten together again?"

Instead of answering directly, he asked, "Why is that important to you?"

She shrugged. "I guess I'm old-fashioned. I think the woman is better off if the man at least feels that he's been the aggressor."

The smile he gave her threatened to shatter her composure. "And you think I might not?"

"It had occurred to me," she admitted.

"There are all kinds of ways for a man to get what he's set his mind to, Cara. One of the best is to give a woman enough room so that she doesn't feel pressured. It comes under the heading of getting her to come to you."

"That sounds so cold-blooded," she protested.

"The opposite. But to answer your original question, yes, if you hadn't called me, I would have called you. I wouldn't have had much choice because I couldn't stop thinking about you." He ran a finger lightly over the soft line of her mouth. "I still can't."

"Your family," she murmured, tasting him against her lips, "they're presuming a lot about us."

"True, but I have the definite feeling that they aren't far wrong."

She was reassured enough by that to enjoy the rest of the evening. In honor of Maria and Joseph's anniversary, there was a huge cake, which they cut amid much laughter and teasing about how much they looked like newlyweds. Everyone had brought presents, but the most impressive was clearly the stereo from their sons. Joseph was especially delighted, and he wasted no time trying it out. As the soaring voice of Luciano Pavarotti singing an aria from *Aïda* filled the room, champagne corks popped, and Mark stood to offer a toast.

"To our parents," he said quietly. "They brought us into the world and they did a great job of raising us to live in it. But if they hadn't given us anything else, what they taught us about love would have been enough. It's the castle they've built together over forty years, and I hope they share it forever."

When he finished his mother's eyes were damp, and even his father's looked suspiciously moist. Cara stood slightly apart from the family, watching them and thinking that she could ask for nothing more but that some day a child would say the same thing about herself and Mark.

But she was a realist and she understood that, whatever the feelings they shared, the future offered no guarantees. Though she tried to minimize the differences between them, she knew they were real and at least potentially a problem. Mark did come from a completely different world, but not for the reason he thought.

Money had nothing to do with it. He was rich in a way she had never known, rich in love. He had grown up with it and was comfortable in both giving and receiving it. He even had the courage to express his love without prompting, something she believed relatively few men could do.

She, on the other hand, had no such background to draw on. For her, love was a mysterious emotion, complex and threatening. Though she cherished every moment she had with Mark, she was also afraid that the whole shining edifice of hopes and dreams she was beginning to construct would come tumbling down and leave her crushed beneath the ruins.

Chapter 9

A nice bit of bacon, Miss," Mr. Mallone said as he reached into the meat case. "From Ireland, it is. Very choice."

"Slice it thin, please," Cara said, shifting her basket from one hand to the other. She had stopped at the store on the way home from working at the crisis hot line, and Mr. Mallone had just been opening up when she arrived. She could see that he was curious about why she was out at such an early hour, but he resisted the urge to ask her.

It had occurred to her in between phone calls that she had never cooked breakfast for a man. At the grand old age of twenty-eight that seemed a singular omission which needed to be remedied as speedily as possible. She and Mark were going out to dinner that evening, and she was far too candid with herself not to expect that he would be spending the night, which meant that, come morning, she could regale him with her culinary expertise.

"Would you have any fresh blueberries?" she asked Mr. Mallone as he handed her the bacon.

He shook his head regretfully. "It isn't the season for them, but the canned ones are very good."

Cara settled for those, picked up a few other ingredients and made her way to the cash register. Mizzus regarded her with interest. "You're up and about early today, Miss Herrington."

"I worked late last night, Mrs. Mallone."

"Indeed." Thinly plucked eyebrows rose in surprise. "That's right, you did mention something about having a job. Some charity or other, if I remember correctly."

Cara suppressed her annoyance at the woman's skepticism, realizing that many people found it hard to believe that she really worked. But she couldn't quite prevent herself from saying, "I was manning a phone at the Downtown Crisis Center last night, Mrs. Mallone. You've pointed out many times what a tough place the world can be, so I'm sure you'll understand why people need help at all hours of the day or night."

"Fakers, if you ask me," Mrs. Mallone sniffed. "Crybabies who can't handle their own problems and want to put them off on somebody else."

"I don't agree," Cara said quietly. "There's nothing wrong with asking for help."

"Help?" the other woman repeated. "They want a handout, that's all. Why, I've been working since I was fourteen and I've never looked to anyone to give me something I haven't earned."

"I'm sure you haven't," Cara murmured, unloading the last of her purchases. Mrs. Mallone seemed more inclined to lecture her than to ring them up.

"That's the trouble with people today," she went on. "No backbone. Why, I said to the Mister, it's a disgrace in this town how people don't want to work. Do you know, we've been trying to hire another stock boy for a month and no one we'd even consider having in the store has so much as applied."

"I'm sorry to hear that," Cara said, pointedly opening a paper bag to pack her items, in the hope that Mrs. Mallone would take the hint. She did, reluctantly.

As her plump fingers punched the cash register keys, she leaned forward and whispered, "We're not too happy with Raymond. He's gotten unreliable. That's why we're looking for someone else."

"That's too bad," Cara murmured.

"If you hear of anyone..."

"I'll be sure to let you know."

She paid what she owed, picked up her bag and turned to leave the store. Near the entrance, Raymond was busy shelving cans of soda. He smiled and held the door for her as he wished her a pleasant day.

After a few hours sleep, Cara went into the office. Diana had warned her that the paperwork was piling up, and that proved to be no exaggeration. It took her most of the afternoon to slough her way through the stacks on her desk. When she finally signed her name to the last letter and shoved it aside, she breathed a sigh of relief.

Diana looked up from her own work and gave her an indulgent smile. "What's got you so tired these days? If I didn't know better, I'd think you were burning the candle at both ends."

"What makes you think I'm not?" Cara asked as she stretched her arms over her head to get out the kinks between her shoulder blades. "You know I've been working on the hot line."

"True, but you should still be getting more sleep than you seem to be."

"Well . . . the fact is I've met this man."

"You don't say," Diana exclaimed. "Tell me all about him."

"He's a cop."

"A what?"

"You heard me, a cop."

Diana shook her head. "Cara, honey, please don't mind me saying this, but you've got to know that going out with cops is a bad idea."

"How come?"

"'Cause they're married to their jobs, that's why. A friend of mine was so far gone on a guy she met that she said it didn't matter if he was on the force. The broken dates didn't matter, the nightmares didn't matter, even the feeling she had that she never really had his complete attention was okay. That's how crazy she was about him."

"What happened?" Cara asked, though she had the definite feeling she didn't want to know.

"They got married, had a baby, bought a nice house out on Long Island. I was just starting to think that I'd been wrong, that everything was going to be all right for her, when he went into a dark alley after some mugger and got himself shot."

"Oh, God . . ."

"It happens, Cara, more often than anyone wants to think about. This is a real dangerous town for cops."

"Mark is careful—"

"That's why he's still alive, but do you really want to have to be worrying about him every time he walks out the door?"

"Anyone can run into a problem, have an accident..."

"Sure they can," Diana agreed. "But a cop goes looking for trouble, that's his job, and more often than not, he finds it."

Slowly, Cara shook her head. "I know you're right. I've thought and thought about exactly what you're saying. But I can't seem to help myself."

"Sounds like you've got it bad."

Cara smiled ruefully. "I'm afraid you're right."

"Well, then," Diana said gently, "guess you'll just have to hope for the best. After all, how often does a man come along who makes you really care?"

"Not very. In fact, it's never happened to me before."

"Then you might as well enjoy it, honey, at least for as long as it lasts."

Good advice, Cara thought. If she had been at all a temporary sort of person, she might have been able to follow it. But all her life she had sought for permanency, perhaps because she had so often been denied it. The thought of losing Mark was intolerable to her, yet she realized that it was a very real possibility. But she was reluctant to bring up her fears about his job, sensing that to do so would be to risk driving a wedge between them just when they needed to come even closer to one another.

Instead, over dinner that night, she told him about some of the people she had talked with on the hot line. "They're our regulars," she said. "People who call in once or twice a week. They really only need someone to talk to and we try to oblige, if we aren't too busy."

He nodded and smiled at her gently. "You're really getting involved in this, aren't you?"

"What do you mean?"

"I've noticed that when you talk about the foundation, you're very matter-of-fact. It's clear that you're glad to be able to do what you do, but I get the feeling that you haven't got a tremendous emotional investment in it. But the crisis center is different, probably because it's so much more immediate and personal."

"It is true," Cara said softly, "that when you're simply deciding whether or not to give people money, you can remain above the fray, so to speak. On the hot line, I'm down in the trenches."

"I still have a hard time thinking of you like that," he admitted, "yet I'd be willing to bet you're damn good at it."

"I don't know about that," Cara said with a smile. "By the end of the night, I feel like a limp dishrag."

"I've come off duty more than once feeling the same way."

"I guess it really isn't so different," Cara murmured thoughtfully. "We're both working with people on a very basic level, except that . . ."

"Except what?" he prompted when she broke off.

"I'm insulated by the telephone. There's some distance between me and them. You don't have that."

"I don't want it," he said quietly. "You can't do good police work at arm's length."

"There must be men who do—the administrators, the people in charge."

"A few of them are pretty good," he admitted grudgingly. "But most are just bureaucrats who don't have a clue as to what it's really like out on the streets."

"Couldn't that change," Cara asked, "if a different sort of person went after those jobs?"

"You mean a guy like me?"

"I didn't say..."

"But it's in your mind. Come on, Cara, spell it out. Are you suggesting I should go after a nice, safe, desk job?"

She hadn't started out to do any such thing, but it somehow seemed to be working out that way. "I don't see anything wrong with a job like that," she said finally. "Somebody has to do it, and from what you just said, I have to conclude that a lot of decisions are being made by people who aren't really qualified."

"That's how it's always been."

"Which isn't to say that it has to continue that way."

He was silent for a moment, looking at her. There was a small candle on their table, and by its flickering light she could see that his features were strained. She felt a stab of guilt at having added to the tension of what had undoubtedly been a difficult day. But with it came the conviction that it was better for her to be honest with him than to diminish their relationship through deception.

"I was afraid this would happen," Mark murmured.

"What?"

"My job, that you would have trouble dealing with it."

"Don't you think any woman would?" she challenged.

"Yes, as a matter of fact, I do. That's one of the biggest problems in being a cop. It's very difficult to keep any kind of stable, happy, personal life."

"Difficult, but not impossible."

His expression lightened slightly, though he still looked very cautious. "What do you mean?"

"Only that I'm not some immature girl who didn't understand what she was getting into. You made it perfectly clear from the beginning that your work is very important to you. I accept that. All I'm saying is that it scares me."

He put a hand into the breast pocket of his jacket as he shook his head. "You don't think that's a big deal?"

"Of course it is. I don't like being scared any more than the next person. But I can live with it." She paused, looked at his jacket and said softly, "You quit smoking, remember?"

He withdrew his hand and laughed sheepishly. "I forgot for a second. You're very distracting."

She smiled as the weight of her fear eased slightly. "I should darn well hope so."

They left the restaurant a short time later and walked back to her apartment. The doorman knew Mark by now and went so far as to grant him a grudging nod. "I've really arrived," he murmured as they got into the elevator.

"What do you mean?" she asked absently, caught up in the now-familiar pleasure of simply being near him, and of knowing that soon she would be even nearer.

"The doorman. He's stopped looking at me as though I were some kind of small-time hood."

"Is that what he did?" she asked with a smile.

"Definitely. I'm sure he counted the doorknobs after I left."

She was still smiling as he put an arm around her waist and drew her against him. His body was warm and hard. She breathed in the clean scent of him and closed her eyes in heady pleasure.

His mouth nuzzled her throat, sending shivers down her spine. She forgot everything except the sheer, overwhelming need to touch and be touched. Her hands were stroking his back through the rough tweed jacket when the elevator abruptly came to a stop.

"We're here," she murmured regretfully.

"Hmm." His lips nudged apart the sides of her blouse and found the scented hollow in her collarbone.

"We have to get off," she gasped.

His arms tightened, lifting her off her feet, pressing her against him so that she could not mistake the full extent of his arousal.

"Apartment..." she groaned, swept away by her own need. "Bed..."

On that note, the elevator doors opened to reveal a stout lady in a mink coat carrying a small poodle under her arm. She stared at them as they at last, reluctantly, broke apart.

"Pardon us, Mrs. Witherspoon," Cara said, recognizing with a sinking heart the very proper matron who occupied the apartment next to her own. She took Mark's hand, squeezing it hard to get across the idea that he should definitely not laugh, and with as much grace as she could muster, left the elevator.

"Well, I never," the woman murmured behind them. Cara fumbled with her keys, finally got the apartment door opened, and they fell into the room.

"Just the other day," she said as Mark, no longer able to restrain himself, burst out laughing, "she was telling me how refreshing it was to meet a young lady who had some respect for propriety."

"She actually put it that way?" he asked disbelievingly.

Cara nodded firmly. "Absolutely. Mrs. Witherspoon is very big on propriety. For that matter, so are most of the people in this building. I wouldn't be surprised if she makes some general announcement at the next meeting of the board of directors to the effect that I'm living in sin."

"Are you worried about it?" he asked, sobering rapidly.

She shook her head. "Of course not. I know I'm not doing anything wrong, and that's all that matters."

"Still, if they're going to make things unpleasant for you..."

"They won't," she assured him. "I won't let them."

Mark looked unconvinced, but Cara promptly put it out of her mind. She had far more important things to think about. "Thank you for a very pleasant evening," she said, drawing herself up on tiptoe to kiss him lightly on the mouth. "I had a very nice time."

"I'm so glad," he said, wrapping his arms around her again. His hands slid down her back to cup her buttocks and squeeze them gently. "However, I couldn't help noticing that you skipped dessert."

"So did you," she whispered, feeling the heat ignite and spread throughout her body.

"An oversight on both our parts. How about having it now?"

"Sounds good to me."

Cara had never been anyone's dessert before, but she found she enjoyed it thoroughly. So did Mark when the tables were turned, and she leisurely explored his body. He stood it as long as he could before he seized her by the shoulders and with a swift movement, turned her beneath him. His hard, muscled form pressed her into the mattress as he thrust a hair-roughened thigh between hers and inexorably urged them apart.

"Take me into yourself, sweet Cara," he murmured hoarsely against her tumbled hair.

She reached down, caressing him with her hand, touched by awe at the power and heat of him. Not until she realized that she was inadvertently adding to his torment did she relent and slowly draw him within her. He groaned thickly as her body took his full length, her secret, inner muscles clenching around him.

"So tight," he muttered against her breast. Lovingly, he caught her nipple between his teeth and teased it until she cried out. Her fingers clenched in his hair, then she pulled his head upright and gazed directly into his eyes.

"I want you," she said. "All of you, right now." To emphasize her point, she tightened even further around him until he moaned her name and began to move. The rhythmic force of his thrusts carried her higher and higher until she was lost to the world and herself, aware only of him and the overwhelming pleasure he was giving her. Pleasure which she fully returned in the moment of her own fulfillment when he joined with her utterly and found his own completion within her silken depths.

Mark woke to the aromas of sizzling bacon and fresh-perked coffee. Presuming that he was caught in a particularly pleasant dream, he smiled and turned over. His hand reached out across the bed, seeking Cara, only to stop when he realized she wasn't there. He opened his eyes, confirmed that he was alone, and got up. Without bothering to put anything on, he padded down the hallway to the kitchen.

She was standing at the stove, singing softly to herself as she caught the bacon on a fork and lifted it onto a plate covered with paper towels. At the sight of her, he burst out laughing.

"Very fetching," he said.

She turned and grinned at him. "I could say the same for you."

"It's every man's fantasy to find a beautiful woman, wearing nothing but a frilly apron, cooking him breakfast."

"What makes you think this is for you?" she asked, returning to the bacon.

"Sheer faith in your tender mercies," he said, kissing the back of her neck. "No woman would torment a man with fresh-cooked bacon and then deny him a bite. Speaking of which . . ." He nipped gently at her nape and laughed when she jumped. His hands cupped her breasts, the thumbs rubbing leisurely over her nipples, until her head fell back against his shoulder and she moaned softly.

"About the bacon," he said.

"What . . . ?"

"It's burning."

"Oh, darn."

He reached around her, turned off the burner, and lifted her into his arms. "We can eat it later."

"This afternoon," she agreed, "or this evening."

"A midnight snack," he said as he walked back down the hall toward the bedroom, carrying her.

"Cold bacon, yum-yum."

"You never heard of club sandwiches?"

"Good idea. Only one thing . . ."

"What's that?" he murmured, lowering her onto the bed.

"I really had my heart set on cooking you breakfast."

"Tomorrow," he said, "or the next day. We have all the time in the world."

Chapter 10

"How about some coffee?" Zack asked as Cara put down the phone and wearily rubbed the back of her neck. "You look as though you could use it."

"Thanks," she said with a wry smile, accepting the cup he offered. "That last one was rough."

"How so?"

"A woman with three kids, no income of her own, and a husband whose idea of a good time is to get drunk and beat her up."

"What did you tell her?" Zack asked.

"I gave her the name and number of a safe house where she could stay with her children while she gets on her feet."

"Do you think she'll go there?"

"Who knows?" Cara said. She took a sip of the hot, bitter coffee and grimaced, not so much at its taste, which she no longer noticed, but at the memory of the just-concluded call. "She's scared to death of what he'll do if she tries to get away."

"Until she gets past that, she's trapped, and so are her kids."

"I tried to make her see that, but I'm not sure I got through."

"You did the best you could," he said reassuringly. "That's all anyone can ask."

Cara knew he was right, but it was still very hard to hang up the phone not knowing what the outcome would be. For a brief time, she had touched another person's life in a very intense way and had her own touched in the process. She could only hope that something good would come of it.

"Maybe she'll call back," she murmured. Along with all the other staffers on the hot line, she gave her first name to callers, though never her last. That was a hard and fast rule. A caller could request a specific counselor any number of times by using a first name, but they were never to be given any information that would allow them to find that person away from the crisis center.

When the rule had first been explained to Cara, she had thought it rather excessive. On reflection, however, she had decided it was merely prudent. The telephone was an open conduit for all elements of society. While the vast majority of people using it were completely decent, all it would take would be one or two who weren't to cause untold trouble.

The phone rang. Cara reached for it and a moment later was immersed in the problems of a teenage girl who felt at war with her parents. She did what she could for her and took a dozen or so additional calls before finally going off duty.

After a brief rest at her apartment, she went to her office to find the usual pile of mail awaiting her. "You're too popular," Diana said as she handed Cara her phone messages.

"I'm on too many mailing lists," Cara murmured. "Would you look at this? Would anyone seriously buy 'a complete set of ceramic birds of prey shipped every month at the incredibly low cost of only $19.95 each?' I know what H. L. Mencken said about no one ever going broke by underestimating the taste of the public, but that's ridiculous."

"Oh, I don't know," Diana said, "I can think of a couple of people that would make a nice gift for."

Cara grinned and shook her head. "Your ex-husband wouldn't be one of them, would he?"

"That fool? I wouldn't waste the time of day on him."

Remembering a time when Diana had been devastated by her divorce, Cara was glad to hear that. She went back to the mail, flipping most of it into the wastebasket, until she came upon a thick, embossed envelope engraved with the name of one Muffy Ste. Martin. A soft groan escaped her.

"Something wrong?" Diana asked.

"Muffy's after me again."

"That girl doesn't give up."

"Another charity ball. This one's for— Oh, no, I don't believe this."

"Let me guess. It's for an artist who specializes in ceramic birds of prey."

"Almost. It's to fund what sounds like a retirement home for over-the-hill show horses."

"You're making that up," Diana insisted.

"I swear, look." She held out the invitation to a dinner dance for the benefit of the Golden Years Equine Association to be held at the Plaza Hotel that weekend.

"She's not giving you much notice, is she?"

"I probably wasn't on the 'A' list," Cara said.

"What's that mean?"

"First she invites the people she wants, counts up how many acceptances she gets, then asks those she could live without to make up the difference. You can always tell which list you're on by how far in advance you get invited. By the looks of this, I'm a 'C' or a 'D' with Muffy."

"Do you care?" Diana asked.

Cara thought about that for a moment and frowned. "Only in so far as it affects my dealings with the people I occasionally ask to help support one of the foundation's projects. It's really not a good idea to be on the outs with too many of them."

"Sounds like you'll have to go then," Diana said, handing the invitation back to her.

Cara took it reluctantly. "I'm afraid you may be right."

"Hey, it won't be so bad. Why don't you get Mark to go with you? Maybe you'll have a good time."

Mark. She hadn't thought about the problem he might present. Given what she knew to be his basic attitude toward rich people, she could think of few events he would be less eager to attend. Yet he would probably take it amiss if she went without him, much less if she asked some other man to accompany her.

"I guess I'll at least have to see if he wants to go," she said reluctantly. "Boy, is this turning out to be some great day. I should have stayed in bed."

"Can't imagine what would have kept you there," Diana said with a suggestive smile.

"Never mind, just do me a favor and call Muffy to let her know I'm going. The last thing I need is to talk to her right now."

"Last time I talked to her, she did ten minutes telling me how Martin Luther King was a real credit to his race. I just love that kind of person."

"Be gentle," Cara requested. "Stupidity can be congenital among the very rich."

While Diana put through the call, Cara resisted the impulse to eavesdrop and picked up her phone instead. She tried to reach Mark without success. He had already left his apartment, and she didn't want to bother him at work. She would be seeing him that evening anyway; he was cooking dinner for her.

Promptly at seven p.m., as had been arranged, Cara arrived at Mark's door. He had offered to pick her up, but she had insisted that wasn't necessary. Instead, she had gone home from work, showered and changed, and then debated whether or not to take a few things with her.

It seemed silly to pretend she wouldn't be spending the night, but on the other hand she didn't feel comfortable showing up with a small suitcase. Muttering to herself about how much easier it was for a man, who could always stick a disposable razor in his back pocket and feel ready to face the world, she tossed one or two items in her purse and was done with it.

As she rang the apartment bell, she told herself there was no reason to be nervous. It wasn't as though this was a first date. They were lovers, after all, and in all likelihood headed toward a great deal more. What was the big deal about going to his apartment?

The moment he opened the door, she knew that it had been wrong to even try to underestimate the evening's importance. Mark was showing her a side of himself she hadn't yet seen.

He stood there wearing a white chef's apron over his shirt and slacks. As always, she felt a spurt of excitement at the mere sight of him. His hair was slightly mussed, and a lock of it fell across his forehead. There was a small nick on his chin where he had cut himself shaving, but it was the trace of flour on his cheek that made her smile. Nervousness fled as, with what could only be described as a proprietorial air, she reached up and gently brushed the flour away. "It's good to see you," she murmured.

"Same here." He kicked the door shut as he took her into his arms and kissed her thoroughly. They could have gone on quite happily in that vein if the oven timer hadn't suddenly emitted a sharp beep.

Mark muttered something under his breath and let her go. "If I hadn't spent so much time on dinner, I'd suggest forgetting it."

"If it didn't smell so good," she countered, "I might go along with you." She looked with interest toward the kitchen, the source of a delectable array of aromas. "What is dinner?"

"Cioppino."

"Beg pardon." It sounded as if he'd sneezed.

"It's the Italian version of bouillabaisse, or more correctly, bouillabaisse is the French version of cioppino."

"Whatever it is, it smells great."

"It also needs tending. Keep me company?"

She nodded and followed him into the kitchen. He poured a glass of wine for her before turning his attention to an enormous pot simmering on the stove. As he tasted a spoonful and began correcting the seasoning, Cara asked, "What's in it?"

"Tomatoes, bluefish, scrod, shrimp, mussels, lobster, olive oil, oregano, garlic, red wine and a few other things."

"It sounds wonderful, but you really didn't have to go to so much trouble."

"Actually, I like to cook. Besides, this is easy compared to some other things I've tried."

"Are the...uh...lobsters in there already?" she asked, peering at the pot.

He shook his head. "They go in at the last. Why?"

"No reason, I'd just rather not watch."

He laughed and opened the oven to remove a loaf of freshly baked bread. "It's okay, they've already gone to their reward. I cut them up ahead of time."

"Oh, good," she said with relief. "Well, not good, actually, I feel sorry for the lobsters, but I really do like the way they taste, so I guess I'm being hypocritical. It's like people who eat veal, but don't want to think about how it's raised. Of course, I eat veal, too, so..."

"Cara," he said gently, interrupting her.

"What?"

"There's nothing to be nervous about."

She took a sip of her wine and tried looking very confident. "Of course not. I'm not nervous at all."

"Really?" He gave her a gently skeptical smile.

"Well, maybe just a little."

"A funny thing happened when you rang the doorbell. For just a second I was actually scared."

"Why?" she asked, genuinely astonished.

"I thought maybe you'd come in here, look around and decide you didn't like the place. After all, a person's apartment says something about them."

In fact, Cara had barely glanced at her surroundings, so caught up was she in merely being there. But now she did so, and immediately liked what she saw. The kitchen was smaller than her own but well proportioned, with a high ceiling and plenty of cabinet and counter space. From where she stood she could see the entry hall, which was lined with floor-to-ceiling bookshelves. Beyond it was a living room with a fireplace and tall windows looking out onto Columbus Avenue.

"You read a lot," Cara said, rather unnecessarily. The apartment was tidy enough, but there were stacks of books and magazines on a table facing the fireplace. More books were stacked on shelves in the kitchen. Counting those in the entry hall, there had to be at least several hundred books in residence.

"They're my one real vice," he said. "Some months I spend more on books than I do on food."

"Going to the library doesn't appeal to you?"

"Sure, that's fine. But there's something about owning a book that makes it almost like a friend." He shrugged a bit abashedly.

"Have you always read?" she asked, looking down into her wineglass.

"Since I was about six. Why?"

"I had trouble learning. My teachers thought I was stupid."

He looked surprised, then pained as though an echo of her sorrow as a child had worked its way into him. "What did your mother do?"

"Nothing." Cara put down her wineglass and looked away from him. "She drank. That's why she and my father divorced. She was waiting tables at a roadside diner in New Jersey when he drove in one night with some of his friends. They were on their way back to the city from a late party at a house in Saddle River. His friends went on, he stayed. They were married three months later when she found out she was pregnant."

"How long did they stay together?"

"Another three months. Even before I was born, they knew they'd made a terrible mistake. In some ways, they were just too different for them to have any chance of making a life together. But in other ways, they were too much alike. They brought out the worst in each other."

"So she left," Mark said quietly, "and went to Texas?"

Cara nodded, still not looking at him. "She was from there and thought her family might help her. They did, grudgingly. By the time I started to school, she was drinking too much to work. We were on welfare most of the time, except when she brought some man home and he stayed for a while."

Mark's hands clenched at his sides. He wanted desperately to reach out to her, to take her in his arms and offer her whatever comfort he could. But he sensed it would not be enough. Right then she needed to say the ugly, painful words that had been bottled up inside her for so long. "Where was your father while all this was going on?" he forced himself to ask.

"All over—New York, London, the Riviera. I remember one time she showed me a clipping from a magazine that had a picture of him on safari in Africa.'' She smiled wanly. "He lived the life of a very rich man who never needed to do anything except satisfy his own whims.''

"Did you ever meet him?''

"Once, when my mother died. I was thirteen then and when he didn't come to the funeral I got so angry that I took the money I'd saved from my after-school job and hopped on a bus to New York. It took three days and three nights, but I finally got here.'' She shook her head ruefully at the memory. "For once, he happened to be in town. I'd found his address on a scrap of paper my mother had saved and I went to his apartment.''

"The one you're living in now?''

Cara shook her head. "No, he bought that later, otherwise I'd have sold it. Anyway, I managed to get there on a day when the butler was off. He answered the door himself and when I told him who I was, he even let me in.''

"Nice guy," Mark muttered. "What did you say to him?''

"I can't remember.'' Which was true. She'd had a speech carefully planned, but she was certain she had never delivered it. "I think I may have asked him why he never came to see me.''

"What did he say?''

"Nothing, really. He took me into the library, offered me a chair, and said he had been sorry to hear about my mother. Then he wrote me a check. As he handed it to me he said he hoped I would understand that he had nothing else to give me and that, at any rate, I was better off not having him in my life.''

"Hell of a thing to say to a kid.''

"But it was the truth. I couldn't even hate him after that. I looked at him, saw that he was as hurt and mixed up as my mother had been, and realized that he was right. I was better off on my own. So I took the check, thanked him and left. I was planning to take the bus home, but when I saw the size of the check, I flew instead."

"It didn't occur to you not to accept it?" Mark asked.

She smiled and shook her head. "Only for about two seconds. It's a hard scrabble growing up poor in Texas. Anyone who does it knows money and romantic notions don't go together. I took it for what it was, and I put it to good use, namely on my education."

"Did you ever hear from him again?"

"Only indirectly, through his attorneys after he died. I'm sure you can imagine my surprise at learning that he had left me his entire estate. Not to mention how shocked I was when I discovered what it amounted to. I'd just presumed he would have drunk it all away before then, but money has a life of its own. Given any chance at all, it keeps on growing. But I've gone on too long. I didn't mean to distract you from dinner."

"That's okay," he assured her quickly. "I'm glad you finally opened up. It must have been tough."

She went to him and touched a light kiss to his cheek. "Actually, it feels pretty good. Now we can get on to better things."

Mark was all for that, though he had to admit, if only to himself, that he would always cherish what had transpired in the past few minutes. He had a greatly heightened sense of intimacy with Cara now that had nothing to do with their sexual relationship. Impor-

tant as that was, there were other things that counted
for more. He was beginning to realize that chief
among those was the trust that made it possible for
them to drop their masks with each other and reveal
their most private selves.

Over dinner, he said to her, "All the things you
do—running the foundation, working at the crisis
center—they're your way of putting your father's leg-
acy to good use, aren't they?"

"That's part of it," she agreed. "But I think I may
also be trying to make a point, namely that money
doesn't have to be a license for self-indulgence, something that becomes tremendously damaging to the
person who has it. Money isn't good or bad by itself;
the use to which it's put determines its character.

"Which reminds me," she added, "I have a favor
to ask."

"Name it."

"I'd like you to attend a charity ball with me."

At the look on his face, she burst out laughing.
"Hey, it won't be that bad. They'll have good food
and a terrific orchestra. These things always do."

"What's the charity?"

"Uh . . . it has to do with animals."

"Baby seals, whales, that sort of thing?"

"Not exactly," she said. "Horses."

"I like horses."

"See, I told you, you'll have a great time."

Mark remained skeptical, but he did agree to go. If
for no other reason, he thought it was time to show her
that he could be as comfortable in her world as she was
learning to be in his.

"By the way," he said as they were clearing the
dishes away, "my folks asked to be remembered to

you. They thought it would be nice if we joined them for dinner one evening soon."

"Does that mean they liked me?" she asked him with a smile.

He grinned back. "Only to the extent of my mother taking twenty minutes on the phone yesterday to tell me how terrific you are and how I'd have to be crazy to let you get away."

"Oh, Lord, you shouldn't have told me that," she said.

"Why not?"

"Because now I'll be nervous about meeting her all over again for fear that she might change her mind."

"No chance, but even if she did, it wouldn't make any difference. I love you, Cara, and nothing my family or anyone else could do can change that one bit."

She blinked against the sudden dampness of her eyes and went into his arms. The dishes were forgotten as they attended to far more important matters.

Chapter 11

Several nights later, as Cara sat at her accustomed place at the crisis center, everything seemed to be going as usual. If anything, it was a little quiet that evening. Enough so for one of the staffers to be knitting while she softly chatted with another. A third was reading up for a course he was taking, and a fourth was writing a letter. They broke off as calls came in, but instead of the continuous stream that occurred some nights, the phones rang only at comfortable intervals.

She was catching up on some paperwork when the phone in front of her rang and she reached for it automatically. "Downtown Crisis Center. This is Cara. May I help you?"

"Cara..."

"Yes, this is she. Have we spoken before?"

"No...not exactly. This is...Joe. I've been...uh...wanting to call for a while."

"I'm glad you did. Is there a particular problem?"

The caller laughed self-consciously. "Yeah, I guess you could say that. The thing is, I'm really hung up on this girl, except I don't think she knows I exist."

Cara frowned. She gathered from the voice that the caller was young, although she wasn't absolutely sure about that because his words were slightly muffled. But whatever his age, advice to the lovelorn wasn't exactly her specialty, or the hot line's purpose.

"Well, Joe, probably the thing to do is to talk to her, see if the two of you have anything in common, that sort of thing."

"It's not that simple."

Somehow, Cara had had the feeling it wouldn't be. She stifled a sigh and summoned her patience. "Is she involved with someone else?"

"I don't know . . . maybe. She's really beautiful."

"Perhaps you could try becoming friends with her and seeing where that might lead."

"I'm not really interested in being her friend."

"That's too bad," Cara said. She was being rapidly put off by the caller's suggestive tone. Zack and Philip had both warned her when she started working at the center that every once in a while, someone with sexual hang-ups called. Both men felt that it was best to cut such people off immediately.

"Listen, Joe," she said briskly, "there's another call I have to take. Just think about what I suggested, all right? Everyone needs friends."

He mumbled something that she chose to take as acquiescence, and she hung up before he could go any further. The phone rang a moment later, and she was quickly involved. Before the night was over, she had forgotten all about Joe.

The following day was Saturday. Cara broke down and went to a Fifth Avenue hair salon for a haircut, the price of which left her gasping. Despite her affluence, she couldn't get over paying close to a hundred dollars for what had cost her twenty-five at most back in Texas. Especially when, try as she might, she couldn't see much difference in the results.

The dress she had chosen to wear, however, was another matter. She had gone all out, buying an absolutely gorgeous couturier original that she lost her heart to before she even looked at the price tag. Which was just as well, since she wasn't sure she could have stood the strain of trying to talk herself out of it.

"I can always be buried in it," she had murmured as the saleslady adjusted the skirt. The woman, who behaved as if she were expecting a call from Buckingham Palace requesting a lady-in-waiting to the Queen, had smiled coldly and assured "madam" that the dress was an absolute steal.

Cara had to go along with that, though she suspected they would have disagreed about who was doing the stealing. Nevertheless, as she stood in front of the full-length mirror in her bedroom, surveying herself, she decided that the extravagance had been worthwhile. A "C" or a "D" she might be to Muffy Ste. Martin, but she was going to be a "Triple A" to Mark.

The expression on his face the moment she opened her apartment door to him made it clear that he thought so, too. His eyes widened before the lids dropped sensuously. He stepped forward, kissed her full mouth, and stepped back to look her over again. The black velvet bodice of her dress was cut low enough to reveal the creamy curve of her breasts. It clung to the narrow span of her waist before flaring out into a black lace skirt that reached her ankles. When she spun around to give him the full effect of the skirt, he saw that her slender back was completely bare.

"Do we really have to go to this thing?" he asked when she faced him again.

She laughed even as her own eyes drank him in hungrily. For a man who undoubtedly had little opportunity to wear a tuxedo, he looked as though he had been born to it. The rigorously elegant apparel only heightened his rugged masculinity. Though both were dressed in black, they were still a study in contrasts. Beside his dark strength she was all light fragility.

"I'm afraid we do," she said softly, "but we don't have to stay too late."

"Good," he growled and opened the door again.

"Wouldn't you like a drink first? We have some time."

He turned and looked at her again, his eyes falling to her breasts and beyond. His mouth was a hard, firm line as he said, "If we're going to leave, it had better be now."

Cara flushed slightly, but went to get her purse. On one level, she was delighted that he desired her so much. But on another, she was faintly distressed by the fierceness of his passion, even though she knew perfectly well that her own matched it. Anticipation was a great heightener of pleasure, but that was hardly necessary in their case. It promised to be a long evening.

It was beginning to snow lightly as they left her apartment house, an unusual event for New York before Thanksgiving. They took a cab downtown to the Plaza Hotel.

"This is one of my favorite places," Cara said as they walked up the marble steps to the main entrance. "There's something so...comforting about it."

"That's an odd word to choose," Mark commented. Inside, the vestibule was crowded with elegantly dressed men and women, some headed for the same charity function they were, others on their way to events scattered all over the city. Beyond, under the high ceiling of the main lobby, the Palm Court was crowded. The tables set amid the potted plants that gave the place its name were occupied by couples and parties having a predinner or pretheater drink.

"Look at them," Cara said softly. "Everyone here looks as though they belong. They've all been here before, probably more times than they can count. Over the years, they've met their friends here, gone to parties, stayed for a night or a week. I met a woman at one of these things who told me that her family from Oklahoma made a point of spending a week every year at the Plaza, and since she's grown up, she comes every few months. This is their idea of New York, and they love it."

"I've got news for them," Mark muttered. "There's a whole other city out there."

"It doesn't matter, this and the few other places like it are a private world."

"The passport to which is money."

"That's right," Cara agreed. "Money and the ability to appreciate this way of life."

"Do you?" he asked as they walked around the side of the Palm Court toward the elevators.

"Appreciate it? Of course, I do. I'd have to be crazy not to like this. It's elegant, serene, luxurious. You come here, and people pamper you, make you feel important and cared for. Who wouldn't respond to that?"

"I have to admit I could stand it every once in a while," Mark acknowledged with a grin. "But not as a steady diet. I prefer to stay more closely connected to reality."

"So do I," Cara said. "That's why I can only take this in small doses, sort of like eating a super rich brownie. It's wonderful while it lasts, but overdo it and you pay the price."

They got off the elevator and joined the throng heading into the ballroom. The strains of a string orchestra reached them from beyond the open double doors. Sleek, tanned women, bedecked in jewels, were touching cheeks and throwing little kisses into the air as they found their friends. The men with them—equally tanned if not as sleek—greeted each other jovially. Everyone seemed, as Cara had predicted, to know everyone else. They might have been all together at a party the previous night and be simply picking up where they had left off, as in fact was often the case.

"There's Muffy Ste. Martin," Cara said, inclining her head toward the dais. "She's the one in pink."

"That's...uh...quite a dress she almost has on," Mark murmured.

"Muffy thinks a woman should look like a woman," Cara explained, tongue firmly in cheek.

"Not much chance of mistaking her for a man," he agreed. "Does Dolly Parton know about her?"

"I hope not. I'd hate for Miss Parton to feel inadequate."

He shook his head ruefully. "I should really try to resist asking this, but are they for real?"

"I don't know," Cara said. "There's a great deal of speculation about that in certain circles. It seems those with less than kind hearts have accused Muffy of resorting to a little surgical aggrandizement."

"That must have run amok. At the risk of exposing my ignorance, I thought flat chests were fashionable."

Before Cara could comment on that, their hostess spied them and raised a hand to wave, causing all those around her to hold their breath in anticipation for a moment.

"Cara, dear," she called, "so nice that you could come to my little affair. And who," she went on, eyeing Mark appreciatively, "is this delicious man?"

Seen closer up, Muffy looked less the twenty-five she strove for and more the forty she would never admit to. The skin around her eyes and mouth was tightly drawn. Her smile was brittle, and there was a too-bright glitter in her eyes. She had the perpetually dissatisfied look of a woman who never quite allowed herself enough to eat, preferring her calories in liquid form.

Cara did the honors as Mark held out his hand. She couldn't help but notice that he flinched slightly when Muffy took it. Her fingers ended in exaggeratedly long nails, which were painted red and slightly curved, giving them the look of talons.

"Let me guess," she said as she looked him up and down as though eyeing her next meal. "You're an investment banker. You have just that look about you."

Since several gentlemen of that profession had recently been sentenced to long prison terms for insider trading, Mark wasn't absolutely sure how to take that. He chose to brush it off. "I'm a detective, Ms. Ste. Martin."

Muffy retrieved her hand. "A...detective? How...droll. Cara, dear, is he some sort of bodyguard?"

"He's on the New York City police force, Muffy," she explained gently. When their hostess continued to appear bewildered, she felt compelled to add, "You know, those people in the blue uniforms? There are others like them who wear plain clothes. They're the detectives."

A sound escaped from between Mark's tightly pressed lips. He cast Cara a helpless look, warning her that in another instant he wasn't going to be responsible for his behavior.

"If you'll excuse us," Cara said hastily, "I see several people I need to talk with."

She all but dragged Mark away from the befuddled Muffy as he burst out laughing. "Oh, Lord," he said gleefully, "I'm in *The Twilight Zone*. There can't really be people like her, can there?"

"I'm afraid so," Cara murmured. "But not that many. Most of the ones here tonight are all right."

"How do you know?"

"Because it's my business. The foundation doesn't operate strictly on the income from its endowment; we also solicit donations. They represent about forty percent of our budget."

"So you have to be nice to these folks?"

"Let's just say I'm not trying to see how many of them I can get ticked off at me. Anyway, what's wrong with being nice?"

"Nothing," he admitted, though without any enthusiasm. "I just find it hard to believe they're worth the time of day."

Cara suppressed a sigh. The evening certainly wasn't getting off to a good start. He looked bored already and more than ready to leave. "We don't have to stay," she said quietly.

"What's that?"

"We could go. I really don't want you to have a rotten evening because of me."

"You really mean it," he said, surprised.

She nodded. It was suddenly singularly unimportant to her that they stay. She wanted to be out of that place, and alone with him, where only the two of them mattered.

Her yearning must have shown in her eyes for he smiled gently. "Thank you, sweetheart."

"For what?"

"For putting me first. Every once in a while, a guy likes that."

"Oh, Mark," she breathed softly, "don't you know you'll always come first with me?"

Several people passed by them, giving them curious looks that changed to understanding and gentle amusement. For a time they were lost in a world of their own. Only the announcement that it was time to sit down to dinner drew them reluctantly back into the present.

A hundred or so tables had been set up on one side of the ballroom with room at each for six people. Cara and Mark shared a table with a lawyer for one of the major news networks and his wife, and a best-selling novelist and her husband who, it turned out, taught sixth grade for the public school system.

Before the usual sympathetic remarks could be made, Bill Healey said, "It's a rough job, but I wouldn't want to do anything else." He smiled at his wife. "Thanks to Janna, I don't have to."

"I read your last book," Cara said. "It was marvelous. How did you ever learn so much about the international gold trade?"

"Before I started writing," the pleasant, middle-aged woman explained, "I worked in a large bank. To be honest, I thought it was the most boring place in the world, which was one of the reasons I started writing seriously. But now that I look back, I realize that I learned a great deal more than I thought."

"Several policemen have written novels," she added to Mark. "Have you ever thought of it?"

He shook his head. "I'm strictly a reader. Besides, as much as my work means to me, I really try not to take it home, which I imagine I'd have to do in order to write about it."

"I think I've got a rough job," Dave Carter, the lawyer, said, "but when I consider what you guys are up against." He shook his head. "From the stories we hear about the public schools, it sounds as though they aren't all that much different from the streets."

"There are some bad apples," Bill agreed. "But there are also an awful lot of good kids who deserve a chance. That's why I stay in it."

"It's the same with police work," Mark said. "There's a temptation after a while to think that everyone's a crook, but it's important to realize that isn't the case. Most people just want to be left in peace, and they ought to have that right.''

''Unfortunately,'' Cara said quietly, ''there's a big difference between what people should have and what actually happens.''

''Take this kind of thing,'' Dave Carter said. ''Of all the tomfool reasons for a charity—''

''Now, dear,'' his patient wife interrupted, laying a hand on his arm, ''your blood pressure...''

''Are you trying to tell me,'' Mark said with a grin as he waved away the waiter who approached to refill his wineglass, ''that you don't think over-the-hill horses need a nice retirement home?''

''I think every animal should be properly cared for,'' Dave said. ''But that isn't the point. At a rough guess, I'd say that maybe twenty percent of tonight's proceeds will actually go for the horses. The rest got spent right here.'' He stuck his fork in the roast quail with juniper sauce decorating his plate, and made a face.

''If you don't mind my asking,'' Mark said, ''if that's how you feel, why are you here?''

''Good question,'' Bill interjected. ''Maybe Janna can come up with an answer. She's the creative one.''

''You know perfectly well why we're here,'' she said, ''and you know I don't like it any better than you do.'' To the others, she explained, ''There are photographers here from the *New York Times*, the *Daily News*, *USA Today* and so on. With a little luck, tomorrow there'll be photos in them captioned 'novelist Janna Healey and her husband, among the invited guests at the charity bash held last night at the Plaza Hotel.' It's called publicity, and it's the name of the game.''

"My reason for attending is pretty much the same," Dave Carter said glumly. "Several of the big network boys come to these things so their wives can show off their latest getups. It pays to be seen attending along with them."

"How about you, Miss Herrington?" Janna inquired. "Something tells me your devotion to horses isn't why you're here."

"No," Cara acknowledged, "but I'm like the rest of you, I'm here because of my work. The foundation I run is trying to raise money to expand the summer program for poor children in this city. We'd like to be able to get more of them out into the country for at least a couple of weeks each year. Two weeks some place like upstate New York or Connecticut runs one hundred and fifty dollars per child. That includes transportation, lodging, all meals, and clothing. We have to supply that last item because a lot of the kids don't have anything appropriate."

"I take it you aren't talking about riding jodhpurs or tennis whites," Elizabeth Carter said.

Cara shook her head. "Absolutely not. The kids get socks, sneakers, T-shirts, shorts and underwear. In other words, the bare essentials. For a lot of them, those are the first new clothes they've ever had."

"This city has such contrasts in it," Elizabeth murmured. "Children like that and people like..." She glanced around at the other tables and then looked ruefully at her own beringed hands. "People like us."

"Nobody ever said life was fair," Cara pointed out. "All I'm trying to do is even the odds a little."

"It sounds like a good cause to me," Janna said decisively. She looked at her husband, who nodded. "We'll contribute."

"Oh, but I didn't mean..." Cara was embarrassed. She had meant to talk with several of her regular contributors, not impose on people she had never met before. But no one seemed to mind.

"I'm on the committee at the network that picks our charitable contributions," Dave said. He reached into his pocket and extracted his card, which he handed to her. "Send me a letter describing the program, and I should be able to get you a substantial check. In the meantime, I'll add something of my own."

By the end of the evening, when the white chocolate mousse with fresh strawberries was served, Cara had sufficient pledges to feel the evening had been a resounding success. She had no idea how well the horses had made out, but her children were doing fine.

Not only that, but in the cab on the way back to her place, Mark said, "That didn't turn out to be what I'd expected."

"Does that mean you had a better time than you thought you would?"

He gave her a smile and nodded. "I liked those people. They're smart and kind. Besides," he added, his smile turning to a very male grin, "I wouldn't have missed seeing Muffy for the world."

"She didn't think you were too hard to look at either," Cara answered him.

"Until she found out what I did for a living," he pointed out matter-of-factly.

"Do you mind?"

"That an insecure, unhappy woman doesn't think I'm worth her attention? You've got to be kidding." He put an arm around her shoulders and drew her against him. "You're what I care about," he said quietly. His mouth brushed hers with tender provocation. "And when we've gotten through this damn traffic, I'm going to show you how much."

"Do me a favor?"

"Name it."

"Tell the cabby to hurry."

Chapter 12

Cara?" The voice on the other end of the phone was young and muffled. She could barely make it out.

"Yes, this is she."

"Uh...this is Joe. I called the other night, remember?"

Cara stifled a sigh. She had hoped she wouldn't hear from him again, but she wasn't particularly surprised he'd gotten back in touch. "Yes, I remember. You called about the girl."

"I'm still crazy about her."

"Have you talked to her?"

"No...not exactly. Like I said, she doesn't know I'm alive."

"Why not?"

He pondered that for a moment. "Because...I don't live in the same world as she does. She'd be as likely to notice me as she would some ant she happened to step on."

"You must be exaggerating. If she were like that, she wouldn't be a very nice person."

"That's not true! She's wonderful."

"Then she must know you're alive," Cara said patiently. Several of the buttons at the bottom of her phone were lit. It was a busy night. She didn't want to be harsh with Joe, but she couldn't justify spending much more time with him. "It doesn't sound to me as if you're giving her much of a chance, if you won't even talk to her. Maybe if you did, you'd be surprised at how she feels. Anyway, I hope everything will work out for you."

"Thanks, but—"

"I'm sorry," Cara said firmly, "but there really isn't anything else I can suggest to you, and I have several other calls to take, so I have to hang up now."

He was still objecting when she forced herself to disconnect the call and move on to the next. She hated being rude or abrupt with anyone, but his problem was inconsequential compared to so many others. It was also quickly forgotten as other people's concerns enveloped her.

Philip Bradley came by toward the end of her shift. He looked tired, as usual, but he still managed a smile and a few reassuring words for everyone. As soon as he could, he drew her off to one side.

"I'm sorry to put any pressure on you," he said, "but I really need to know if we'll get the funding. The stack of bills on my desk is growing by the day, and our creditors are getting a bit annoyed with us. Somehow I've got to come up with more money."

"You've already done it," Cara said. She had made up her mind earlier that day that the center would get the additional support Philip had asked for. There was no question that it was a well-run organization providing an important service. "I thought you might come by, so I brought the check with me."

When she handed it to him, his eyes widened. He read the amount several times before allowing himself to believe it. "This is twice what I asked for."

"Does that mean you don't think you can use it?" Teasingly, she reached out for the check. "I can write you a smaller one."

"Oh, no," he said, laughing as he held the check out of her reach. "This one is just fine. We'll be able to put in more phone lines, start some in-person counseling, maybe even expand our facilities. I was thinking only the other day how great it would be if we could offer more concrete help instead of merely advising people whom to get in touch with. There's a building next door that could be a safe house for women and children. And the church up the block has a meeting room we could use for drug and alcohol counseling. Not only that, but..."

"Whoa," Cara said gently. "Take it easy. You can't do everything at once, especially not as tired as you are. Why don't you think about hiring some administrative help?"

"I have thought about it," he admitted a little sheepishly. "But I hate spending money for anything I could do myself."

"In my experience," Cara said, "no organization can run on strictly volunteer help after it grows beyond a certain size. You're in the process of doing that. It's time to recognize it and respond accordingly."

"I'll think about it," he promised, "and thanks. You saved us."

"If I hadn't come along, someone else would have. You deserve to keep going."

"People don't always get what they deserve," he said somberly. A thought suddenly occurred to him. "Hey, this doesn't mean you'll be leaving, does it?"

"Well...the idea was for me to work here for a while to get a better feel for the place. I've done that and there are other things..."

"You've also turned into one of our best counselors. I'd hate like anything to lose you."

"I appreciate that," she said sincerely. The fact was she hated the idea of leaving the center. Hard and often draining as the work was, it made her feel as though she were helping with more than just money. "Maybe I could stay on for a while..."

"Great," he said before she could change her mind. "Hey, everybody, Cara's staying!"

The other counselors looked up from their calls, saw that Philip was happy about something, and gave a little cheer. Cara gave him a chiding look. "I said for a while. You made it sound permanent."

"What's permanent," he asked cheerfully, "except a string of whiles one after another? A while here, a while there, pretty soon you're talking about real time."

"Somebody said that about money, too. A billion here, a billion there, pretty soon you're talking about real money."

"The late, great Senator Everett Dirksen," he told her. "He was speaking of government spending. I like to believe it was an ironic reference."

Cara shook her head wryly. "I have to get out of here. There's a definite air of giddiness developing."

Philip walked her to the elevator and couldn't resist giving her a quick hug. "Thanks again," he said. "We'll put every penny to good use."

"That's why you got it," she said as the doors opened and she stepped inside. He was still standing there, looking like a little boy on Christmas morning, when the doors closed again.

As had become her routine, Cara went back to her apartment and slept for a few hours, then got up, showered, dressed, and went into the office. As she was walking toward the foundation's building, she paused at a newsstand to buy a paper. As she picked up the paper, the headline screamed at her: Cops Shot on Stakeout. One Dead.

Cara closed her eyes against the sudden dizziness that gripped her. She swayed weakly and had to lean against the side of the newsstand to keep from falling.

"Hey, lady," the newsdealer said, "you okay?"

Cara didn't answer at once. It was all she could do to catch her breath and force herself to look at the headline again. "I..."

"You sick or something?"

"No... I'm sorry..."

The gruff newsdealer looked from her ashen face to the paper she held, then back to her. "Hey," he said more gently, "you married to a cop or something?"

"N-not exactly..."

"Terrible thing," he went on, ignoring her disclaimer. Talking around the cigar stub in his mouth, he said, "It always makes me mad when one of those guys gets it. Remember the one a year or so ago, he was six months away from retirement, had a wife and several kids. Went out on a routine call and—'' he made a gun of his index finger and pretended to shoot it ''—bam, that's it for him. I'll tell you, this town isn't what it used to be....''

''I have to go,'' Cara said weakly. She dropped the paper and hurried away.

She had no memory of walking the remaining blocks to her office or of dropping into her chair without responding to Diana's greeting. Not until she saw the other woman bending over her, a cup of water in her hand and a deeply concerned look on her face, did she realize how oddly she was behaving.

''I'm fine,'' she said quickly. ''I just had a bit of a shock.''

''You looked as though you'd been hit by a truck,'' her friend said. ''What on earth happened?''

''There was...'' She paused, took a sip of the water, and forced herself to breathe deeply. ''There was a headline in the paper about cops being shot. It shook me up. It's silly,'' she went on hurriedly. ''I'm terribly sorry about what happened, but there's no reason to think Mark was in any way involved.'' She remembered then about dropping the paper and wondered whether or not to regret that.

''Of course not,'' Diana said briskly. ''There are thousands of police in this city. Why don't you just stay where you are, and I'll fix you a nice cup of tea. Won't be but a minute.''

She hurried off, and Cara leaned her head back against the chair, letting her eyes close. She really had to get a grip on herself. If this was how she reacted to the mere thought of him being hurt, how would she ever manage if...

''Cara.'' At Diana's soft voice, she opened her eyes and sat up. One look at her face, and she had a horrible idea of what she was about to hear. "I turned on the radio while I was making the tea. It was two homicide detectives who were shot. One of them's dead."

"Oh, God, please..."

Diana was instantly at her side. She put her arms around her and held Cara gently. "It's okay, honey," she said softly. "It's okay. There's got to be somebody you can call, right? Somebody who'll know where he is? Probably won't take more than a couple of minutes to clear this up."

"He gave me a number," Cara murmured. She reached down for her purse, opened it, and fumbled for a slip of paper tucked into her address book. Her hand was shaking so badly as she drew it out that she almost dropped it.

"I'll dial it," Diana said quickly, taking the paper. She went around to the other side of the desk, picked up the receiver, and punched in the number. It rang several times before being answered. Diana handed the receiver to Cara, but stayed nearby.

Unsure of how to begin, Cara said the first thing that came into her mind. "Is Mark there? Mark Sabatini?"

The man on the other end of the phone sounded very cautious as he asked, "Who's calling, please?"

"My name is Cara Herrington. I'm...uh...a friend of his. I'm sorry to bother him at work, but I just needed to know if..."

"Please hold on a moment, Ms. Herrington."

A woman's voice came on the line. "Ms. Herrington. This is Officer Haley. Lieutenant Sabatini is out of surgery and doing very well."

"H-he's what...?"

"He's out of surgery and— Oh, I'm sorry, you didn't know." The woman was instantly contrite. "Please forgive me. I thought when you called— Look, he really is okay. It was his partner..." Her voice broke. She coughed and struggled to recover. "His partner, Rory Harrison, who..."

"Please," Cara gasped, "where is Mark?"

The woman named a downtown hospital. "We can send transportation for you, if you like."

"No...I can get there. It's all right...if I come?" Even as she asked the question, she wondered why she was bothering. Nothing on earth could possibly keep her away.

The woman assured her that it was, though she couldn't say when she would be allowed to see Mark. Cara hung up the phone a moment later and sat staring at it.

"I'm so sorry, honey," Diana said softly. "But he's alive...isn't he?"

Cara nodded, trying without success to brush away her tears. "His partner..."

Diana bit her lip. She handed Cara a tissue. "I'll go with you."

The hospital was an old one, located far downtown in a sprawling complex of red brick buildings dating from early in the century. As Cara and Diana got out of the cab that had brought them, an ambulance tore past them toward the emergency entrance.

"They get a lot of business here," the cabby said. "Night and day, it never stops."

Cara didn't reply. With Diana beside her, she walked up the steps to the main entrance. The lobby was crowded; off to one side there was a cluster of plastic chairs, all taken. Men and women of all ages and backgrounds sat talking to one another. Some simply stared off into space with the absent expressions of those whose minds are elsewhere, on the hospital's upper floors, with their loved ones.

Several of those milling around in the lobby were police officers. Some were in uniform, others in plainclothes. They all looked very grim. Diana went up to the desk and spoke with the woman seated there. She came back to Cara quickly. "They say we have to speak to the police administrator in charge. He's over there." She pointed toward a tall, well-built man in a tan overcoat who was talking with several of the officers.

As Cara approached him, he turned, looked at her, and broke off his conversation with the other men. "Ms. Herrington? I'm Pierce Stewart."

"Yes, but how did you . . . ?"

"We've been trying to get in touch with you. You can see Mark now."

"He's . . . all right?" She could hardly dare to believe it; if the man said no . . .

But instead he nodded gently. "He got lucky. The bullet only dented his forehead. He'll be fine."

"Does he know . . . ?"

"About Lieutenant Harrison? Yes, he does. I'm glad you're here. You seem to be the person he most wants to see."

He escorted both Cara and Diana to the elevator, and rode up with them to the fifth floor. A uniformed police officer was standing in the hallway. The administrator nodded to him. "Anything?"

"No, sir," the officer said. "It's quiet."

As Stewart started down the hallway, Cara stopped. He was forced to do the same. She looked at him directly and said, "There's something you haven't told me. What is it?"

Stewart hesitated. Reluctantly, he said, "The man who shot Mark and Rory is still at large. We really don't expect him to be stupid enough to come here, but until he's apprehended we'll be taking some precautions."

"I see...." There were numerous other questions she could have asked him, and more than a few of them occurred to her, but Cara realized that she really didn't want any of the answers. At least not right then. Above all, she wanted and needed to see Mark.

He was lying in the hospital bed, alone in the single room, his eyes closed. Stewart and Diana had remained outside in the hall. Cara shut the door behind her and for a few moments she merely looked at him, taking in the steady rise and fall of his chest, and the other signs that assured her he was whole and alive. His color was not normal, but it wasn't really bad either. There was a stark white bandage around his forehead, but it was neither as big nor as ominous appearing as she had feared.

As she watched, he opened his eyes, looked at her, and wordlessly held out a hand.

She was across the room in an instant, her fingers twining around his. "Oh, Mark," she breathed, "I've been so frightened."

Still dazed by the anesthetic he had been given, he could only mouth a single word: "Sorry."

"No, don't say that. You didn't do anything to be sorry about. I'm only so...so sorry myself about..." She broke off, seeing the pain in his eyes and realizing that the last thing he needed was to be reminded of his partner's fate.

"You have to rest," she said, touching his cheek tenderly. "That's what's most important now. Everything else has to wait."

His lips moved again, stiffly. "Rory..."

"Oh, Mark..." Tears filled her eyes, slipping unheeded down her pale cheeks. She laid her head down beside his and wept. After a few moments, she became aware that he did the same.

The funeral for Rory Harrison was held three days later. Mark insisted on going, against the advice of his doctors who released him from the hospital with great reluctance.

"It's true his wound isn't as serious as it could have been," one of them told Cara, "but that doesn't change the fact that he took a bullet to the skull. He's not going to bounce back from that overnight no matter what he thinks."

"If I had my way," Cara explained quietly, "Mark would stay here until you were all convinced that it was safe for him to leave. But we both know that isn't going to happen. It's very important to his emotional recovery that he be able to pay his respects to his partner."

"I understand that," the doctor said, "and it's the only reason I'm letting him go. Emotional recovery is every bit as important as physical healing, maybe even more so because the mind seems to have an enormous impact on the body. So he can go and do his grieving, but he also has to be sensible and get plenty of rest."

"He will," Cara assured the white-coated man. The grimly determined look in her eyes convinced him that she was right.

But later, as the funeral cortege drew up in front of the small, neighborhood church where the service was being held, Cara wondered at her own wisdom in being there. For Mark, and to a lesser but nonetheless real degree, for his fellow officers, it was an important rite of farewell, a way to honor a colleague and friend. For the others—the spouses, lovers and parents—who were in attendance, it was a frighteningly close look at a tragedy they prayed would never touch them personally.

The muffled beat of drums echoed in Cara's mind as she watched Mark walking behind the casket. For the first time, she saw him in uniform. He wore it well, his bearing erect and proud. But the stark sorrow stamped on his face was an eloquent testament to his inner suffering. Not even the knowledge that the man responsible for his partner's murder and his own shooting had been apprehended could ease his pain. Only time could do that. As the casket passed by her, Cara could only be grateful that for Mark, at least, time still existed.

After the services in the church and the simple graveside ceremony that followed, she waited her turn to say a few words to Linda Harrison, Rory's widow. The need to do so made her uncomfortable. She felt that it was inappropriate for a stranger such as herself to intrude in any way into another woman's grief, and yet it would also have been highly inappropriate to say nothing at all. As she approached the petite, pale woman, she decided to speak simply from her heart.

"I wish I had met your husband," she said quietly after she had introduced herself. "Mark cared a great deal about him. He doesn't care deeply for many people, so Rory must have been someone truly special."

Linda Harrison looked at her carefully for a moment, then a soft smile touched her pale mouth. "He was, and he felt the same way about Mark. They were partners a long time. Bad as this is, I thank God it wasn't both of them."

She hesitated briefly, then added, "You and Mark...?"

Cara didn't need words to understand what she meant; the look in her eyes was enough. Silently, she nodded.

"I won't tell you not to worry," Linda said. "But now that the worst has happened to me, I have to say that I have no regrets. Rory was the man he was precisely because he cared so much. It's a dangerous thing, caring, but absolutely necessary. I'm only grateful I was able to share my life with such a man even if it wasn't for as long as I would have liked."

"I'm not sure that I have your kind of courage," Cara murmured.

Linda touched her hand gently. "It comes with the loving. You'll see." Her eyes met Cara's as she added, "Just be there for Mark now. He really needs you."

Cara nodded. "I'll do anything I possibly can for him." She meant it, but at the same time she worried that the same love that made her yearn to help him also made her terribly afraid of the risks he took simply by being who and what he was. Loving him didn't give her the right to try to change him, but it did make the temptation to try almost irresistible.

Chapter 13

"What's a seven-letter word for xylophone beginning with *m*?" Cara asked, looking up from the crossword puzzle she was assiduously pursuing.

From the couch, where he was stretched out reading, Mark mumbled, "Marimba."

She filled in the letters, saw that they fit, and looked at him admiringly. "How did you know that?"

He put down his book and returned her gaze. "Because I've been doing those damn puzzles until they're coming out of my ears. Not to mention reading everything I can get my hands on and following the other *extremely* limited activities that quack at the hospital said were okay."

"That 'quack' happens to be one of the finest neurosurgeons in the business. You should be grateful he was there to work on you."

"I am, but why he had to go and tell the brass that I needed two weeks of sick leave is beyond me. I tried to convince them he was wrong, but they wouldn't listen.''

"It hasn't done you any harm to take it easy for a while. Besides, you go back to work tomorrow.''

"Not a moment too soon. I couldn't take much more of this.''

At the look that crossed her face, he cursed softly and levered himself off the couch. He was beside her before she could blink. "I'm sorry, sweetheart. That was a really tactless thing for me to say. You've been great, spending so much time with me, putting up with my moods...''

"I wanted to do it,'' she interrupted. "Don't you know how hard it would have been for me to be away from you right after...'' She broke off and averted her eyes, not wanting him to see what was in them.

Mark knelt down before her. Gently but insistently, he cupped her chin in his fingers and turned her head to him. "I could never have gotten through this without you.'' At her disbelieving look, he insisted, "I mean it. Sure, I would have survived, but that would have been it. I wouldn't have come to terms with what happened.''

"Have you?'' she asked gently.

He thought about it for a moment, then nodded. "As much as I possibly can. When it first happened, I was so angry that I scared myself. I wanted to strike out at everyone and everything. But now I realize that Rory understood the risks he was taking, the same as we all do. He made his own choices and somehow I know that wherever he is, he doesn't regret them.''

"Mark...''

"Yes, sweetheart?''

"There's something..." She broke off, caught between the need to say what was in her heart and the conviction that neither the time nor place were right. "Never mind."

"No, tell me. Whatever's worrying you, let it out."

"It's just..." She looked into his dark eyes, seeing the love there and the desire to return to her some measure of the support she had given him. That desire, more even than the love, made him vulnerable. If she asked him for something now, he would be hard-pressed to refuse it.

A faint smile that she knew he would not be able to decipher curved her mouth. Quelling the desperate words clamoring to be heard, she said, "I was just wondering if we might be able to get away together some time soon. Have a little vacation, maybe."

"That's a great idea. I've got plenty of time piled up. Do you have any idea where you'd like to go?"

They spent the next hour or so debating the various merits of the Caribbean versus Hawaii. The discussion continued over dinner at Rudy's and during the walk back to Cara's apartment. It didn't break off until they were in bed together, too distracted by each other to talk.

The next day Mark returned to work and so did Cara. During his two-week convalescence, she had dropped by the office several times to pick up paperwork and confer with Diana, so she didn't feel that she was too badly out of touch. Still, it was with some relief that she settled behind her desk, determined to make a dent in the many matters piled up for her attention. If nothing else, they would keep her from thinking about Mark.

By lunchtime, she had made significant progress, enough to make her feel justified in getting out for half an hour. She went for a brisk walk and returned with her cheeks glowing. As she entered the office, Diana looked up and gestured to the phone.

"Phil Bradley's on line two," she said.

Cara picked up the receiver without bothering to take her coat off. "Hi, Phil, how's it going?"

"Fine, thanks. It's good to have you back. Everything okay?"

She knew what he was asking and appreciated his concern, as much as she did the tact which prevented him from probing any further. Phil was, like just about everybody else in New York, aware of what had happened. She knew that he felt for both her and Mark without having to hear him say so.

"Everything's fine," she assured him. "What's new at the center?"

"We're putting your money to good use, but we miss you. That's why I'm calling. Is there any chance of your coming back for a while?"

Cara hesitated. She had originally planned to continue her work at the center until events intervened to decide otherwise. But now she wasn't so sure whether she should go back or not. "I don't know, Phil.... Things haven't exactly settled down yet."

"I understand, just do me a favor and keep us in mind? We really could use you."

Cara promised she would think about it, but she already suspected that she'd go back to work at the center, at least for a while. There was no reason not to, since Mark usually worked several nights a week pursuing leads. She would wait until he was back on a regular schedule and then she'd call Phil.

The opportunity came a week later. Mark had a new partner who, though he would never take Rory's place, seemed to know his stuff. His name was James Muir. He was a large, steady man who had grown up in Harlem and had joined the police force because he didn't like what he saw happening to his friends. Divorced, he had no children, no pets, and no vices, except, as Mark said, "An uncanny habit of being right. He came up with a lead on those pizza parlor murders that have had us stymied. We're going to check it out this evening. I hope you understand about my not being able to make dinner, but . . ."

Cara assured him that she did understand and resisted the impulse to tell him to be careful. The idea of an evening alone didn't have as much appeal as she would have expected. Always a person who valued her independence, she had become so used to being with Mark that she was at a loss to know what to do on her own. It didn't take her long to decide that her suddenly empty hours could best be spent at the crisis center.

Phil was delighted when he heard, and so were Zack and the others when she arrived. "Good to have you back," Zack told her. He spoke for everyone when he said, "We've missed you."

"Thank you," Cara murmured, looking around at the dozen or so men and women who smiled their greetings. Only then did she realize how much she had missed them. They had become like a family to her and being back among them gave her strength.

Which it seemed she would need. The crisis center was busier than ever. Over the next few hours, the telephones rang constantly. Cara barely had a chance to catch her breath in between calls. She was hardly aware of the passing time and was surprised, when she glanced up at the wall clock, to see that it was after midnight. She was about to get some coffee, when the phone rang yet again and she reached for it.

"Downtown Crisis Center. Cara speaking."

"Cara . . . is that really you?"

"This is Cara. Who's calling, please?"

"This is . . . uh . . . Joe. I've missed you. Where have you been?"

Cara frowned, but managed to keep her tone neutral. "Oh, Joe . . . I've been away the past few weeks."

"I thought it might be something like that, even though I couldn't get anyone to tell me anything. I'm glad you're back."

"Yes, well, so am I. But if there isn't anything else . . ."

"There is! I need to talk to you, more than ever, but it's so hard on the phone. I was wondering if maybe we could meet some place?"

It was an absolute rule of the crisis center that workers never, under any circumstances, agreed to meet callers in person. Cara didn't consider breaking it for a moment. "I'm sorry, but I can't. There are other calls, Joe. I have to go—"

"Wait! Don't just cut me off like that. Damn it, you've been gone for weeks. I haven't been able to talk to you, and now you want to hang up. That isn't right."

She had run out of patience. Kind though she wanted to be, the time had come to be firm. "Joe, I have to be frank with you. The type of problem you have isn't really what we're set up to deal with here. I'm sorry about that, but it's just the way it is."

"Oh, it is, is it?"

About to hang up, Cara hesitated. Something in his voice made her do so. Cautiously, she said, "Yes, there's nothing else I can do."

"People always say that when they're doing something bad."

"I'm not—"

"Yes, you are! You don't care anything about me so you're going to cut me off. But you don't really care about anyone, do you, Miss High-and-Mighty. You're just amusing yourself talking to the lowlifes—"

"That's enough! I'm sorry you're so upset, but—"

"*I'm* upset? Wait until you see how upset you get."

A cold finger of apprehension moved down Cara's back. "What's that supposed to mean?"

"You don't think I'm going to let you get away with this, do you? Pretending to be nice to me and then turning out to be just like all the others. I'll make you pay."

"Joe—"

"No, it's too late to try to make up. I'm going to get you for this, Cara, and when I do, you're going to be very, very sorry."

An instant later the line went dead. Cara was left looking at the phone with a sense of mingled disbelief and apprehension. She told herself that what people said often had little relation to what they did. Making threats was a far cry from carrying them out. But she couldn't shake the sense of fear that had descended on her, which dogged her throughout the rest of the night.

But by the next day, she had succeeded in putting Joe out of her mind. She told herself that he was simply a troubled and unhappy young man who had used her as a way of venting his own frustrations. There was no reason for her to think that she would ever hear from him again. That seemed to be proven true when the next two nights she worked at the center passed uneventfully.

In between, she and Mark spent every possible moment together. One night when he got off work, he stopped by her office to pick her up, and James Muir was with him. The big, somber-faced man nodded politely to Cara, glanced at Diana, and went back for another long, hard look. Diana returned his scrutiny in full measure. They assessed each other warily as Cara and Mark pretended not to watch. At length, James said, "I'll be going uptown now. Care for a lift, Miss Baldwin?"

"I wouldn't mind," Diana said. Under the cover of reaching for her purse, she gave Cara a wink.

"Well," Cara said when the pair had left, "I never. Do you think they'll hit it off?"

"About as well as oil and water," Mark said with a grin. "But shake them up enough and who knows?"

"I suppose people could say the same about us," Cara said as they were leaving the office building.

He took her arm as they crossed the avenue. Traffic was heavy. People were streaming out of all the surrounding buildings, heading down into the subways or across town toward the train and bus terminals. Cars, cabs and buses jockeyed for position as horns blared. Hardened pedestrians, immune to any sense of danger, threaded their way around and between the vehicles.

"I suppose they could," Mark agreed when they reached the other side of the street. Ahead lay Central Park. One of the horse-drawn carriages that were a chief attraction of the park happened by. On impulse, Mark raised a hand to signal the driver.

"Let's go for a ride," he said to Cara.

Side by side in the carriage, snug under a fur blanket, they rode in silence for some time. The rhythmic clip-clop of the horse's hooves was soothing, as was the carriage's gentle sway. A full harvest moon was rising over the bastion of apartment houses to the east. It smiled down benignly at the shadowy trees and winding paths.

"This is like a different world," Cara murmured. Her head lay on Mark's shoulder. Beneath her hand, she could feel the steady beat of his heart. "I can hardly believe I had the scare here that I did."

"It's like everywhere else," Mark said quietly, "not good or bad by itself. The use people make of it determines that."

Cara smiled, her lips brushing the rough tweed of his jacket. "I'd say this is a good use."

He laughed softly and turned so that he could look at her. "I'm glad you think so."

They shared a long and tender kiss that spoke of vastly more than passion. In it was true caring and commitment, a genuine savoring of each other, and a sense of understanding made all the more precious by its rarity.

Both were startled when the driver's discreetly expressionless voice announced that the ride was over.

Mark had planned to cook dinner for both of them, and eventually did, though by the time they thought to eat, it qualified more as a midnight snack.

Cara was halfway through her next shift at the crisis center when Joe called again. She had been so convinced that he wouldn't do so that for a moment she didn't recognize his voice. When she did, she hung up instantly and sat staring at the receiver as though it had suddenly turned into a dangerous animal.

"Something wrong?" Zack asked. He had the seat next to her and had glanced over the low partition separating them in time to see her frightened expression. Though his own tone was calm, he was instantly alert.

"I'm not sure," Cara said shakily.

"What happened?"

Briefly, she explained about Joe's phone calls, ending with the one during which he had threatened her. "I really thought that would be the end of it, but now he's called again."

"And you hung up?"

She nodded. "Right away. I don't know if I did the right thing or not."

"You did," Zack said firmly. He was about to go on when Cara's phone rang again. Uncertain what to do, she looked to him for guidance. "Go on and answer it, but let me pick up at the same time. I can get the same line here." He pushed the necessary button, and together they lifted their receivers.

"You shouldn't have done that," a low, angry voice snarled.

Zack looked over at Cara and mouthed a single word: "Joe?"

She nodded, swallowed hard and forced herself to stay calm. "Do what, Joe?"

"Hang up on me like that. Don't think I don't know you did it. That was a mistake, Cara. Now I really am angry at you."

"You have no reason to be, Joe. I haven't done anything to you."

"Yes, you have! You're like all the others—snobby, thinking you're better than me. Well, you aren't, and I'm going to prove it."

"H-how are you going to do that?"

He laughed unpleasantly. "You'll see, and you won't like it . . . at least not at first."

"W-what are you talk—"

"Hang up," Zack ordered sharply as he did so. When she couldn't respond immediately, he reached over the partition, grabbed her receiver and slammed it down on the phone. His thin face was drawn with concern. "That guy's a nut. You absolutely don't want to have any more contact with him."

"I agree," Cara said. She became aware that she was shaking and wrapped her arms around herself in an effort to stop. "Anyway, after that I don't think he'll call again. He must have heard you and realized that someone was listening in."

"Maybe he'll get the message and maybe he won't." Zack hesitated a moment, then said, "I hate to say this, Cara, but I think you'd better take some time off from here. It's the last thing I want, but your safety comes first."

"You really think it's that bad?"

"I think it's better to err on the side of caution. If he does call back, he'll simply be told you're no longer with the center. That should do it, and after a while you can return. But let's give it a few weeks to be sure."

Reluctantly, Cara agreed. She hated having to change her life in any way because of an anonymous, cowardly threat, but she had to agree with Zack. It was better to be cautious.

* * *

The lead James Muir had come up with on the pizza parlor killings had turned out to be solid, so he and Mark were busy that evening tracking down witnesses. Cara opted for a long bath and a good book. She was curled up with the latest Dick Francis mystery when the phone beside her bed rang.

"Cara?"

"Yes, who—"

"Don't you recognize my voice? It's Joe."

No, Cara thought, it couldn't be. Frantic thoughts raced through her mind. How could he possibly have gotten her phone number? Not only was he not supposed to know her last name but her number was unlisted. There was only one way he could have...

He had to know her.

"Who is this?" she cried. "Who are you?"

"I'm angry at you, Cara. And I'm going to hurt you."

The phone went dead. She was left staring at it as a deadening cold spread over her, for the moment blocking out even her terror.

Chapter 14

Let's try it again," Mark said quietly. "When was the first time he called you?"

"A few weeks ago," Cara said. She was sitting on the couch in her living room. Mark sat next to her. It was the following morning. She had called him as soon as she thought he would be home. He had come over immediately and ever since then they had been going over what had happened.

"I don't remember exactly when the first call was," she explained tiredly. Her eyes burned, and her throat was sore. She felt as though she was coming down with something vile, although she suspected that wasn't the case. Sheer fright and nervous tension were making her feel ill. "We don't keep a log of calls, so there's no way to know for sure."

"All right," Mark said, "let's move on. When he's called, do you remember hearing any sounds in the background? Other voices, for instance, or music, a dog barking, anything like that?"

Cara thought for a moment. Slowly, she said, "I did hear something . . . traffic, I think. Cars going by."

"A pay phone."

"He's making the calls from outside?"

Mark nodded grimly. "That either means he doesn't have ready access to a phone wherever he lives, which is pretty rare these days, or he didn't want to be overheard."

Thinking of all the detective shows she had seen on television, Cara said, "Maybe he didn't want the call to be traced either."

Mark smiled humorlessly. "It's practically impossible to trace calls under any circumstances. The phone system has gotten so complicated that what used to take a few minutes can now go on forever. But he wouldn't necessarily know that."

"I guess that means we can rule out employees of the telephone company," Cara said wanly.

"We're not ruling out anyone," Mark corrected, "except people who were actually with you at the time the calls were received. Now let's go back over the last conversation again."

"Please," Cara said, "we've gone over and over it. We're not going to turn up anything new. He knows who I am; that's what matters."

Recognizing that she was nearing the end of her rope, Mark nodded. "All right, we'll let that go for the time being. Let's concentrate instead on who 'Joe' might be. Any idea of his age?"

"I've already told you," Cara said, her hands twisting in her lap, "he sounds young, but I'm not sure because his voice was always muffled."

"Any sort of accent?"

She shook her head.

"Unusual choice of words?"

"No."

"Personal details?"

"He said there was a girl he cared about who didn't seem to know he existed."

"It's a safe bet he was talking about you. Did he say where he'd seen this girl?"

"No, he said very little, really."

"He's careful, and probably no dummy. Somewhere your path has crossed his, enough for him to know your name and have access to your unlisted number. We need to start making a list of all the males who would fall into that category."

"There can't be that many of them," Cara said.

She was wrong. By the time they had listed all the men she might conceivably have met in the course of any given day and who could have either been given or stumbled across her unlisted number, Mark had filled four pages in his notebook.

"You're a friendly lady," he said with a grim smile when he finally snapped it shut. It was midmorning and they were both hungry. Cara offered to fix breakfast, and he took her up on it.

"I didn't realize," she said as she cracked eggs into a bowl and scrambled them. "But surely at least some of the people on that list don't really belong there. I barely pass the time of day with them."

"Which makes them all the more suspect. The chances are that you don't know 'Joe' very well, otherwise something about him would seem familiar."

"Nothing does," she assured him. "I've racked my brains and I don't have a clue who he could be."

"We'll find him," Mark said as he set the table. They ate largely in silence, until he said, "I want you to pack a bag. You're going to spend a few days at my place."

She looked at him, surprised. "Do you really think that's necessary?"

Instead of answering directly, he posed a question of his own. "Is it such a hardship, staying with me?"

"No, of course not," she assured him hurriedly. "I guess I just resent the idea of being forced out of my own home."

Mark reached across the table and touched her hand gently. "I understand, but you have to be sensible about this. Anyway, it won't be for long."

"You sound very confident."

"I am. No way this guy is staying loose."

His implacable determination both relieved and frightened Cara. She was profoundly glad not to be on the receiving end of it, even as she wondered what exactly he had in mind to do if and when he caught up with "Joe."

Mark didn't enlighten her. Instead, he carried his dishes over to the sink and said, "While you're packing I've got a few calls to make."

As she was sorting through her drawers, trying to decide what to take, she could hear the low rumble of his voice. He had asked her for Phil Bradley's number, along with others, and she supposed that was one of the people he was talking with.

When she emerged from the bedroom carrying her case, he was just hanging up the phone. "Did you reach everyone you wanted?" she asked.

He nodded and came over to take the bag from her. "Bradley knew about the calls to the center. In fact he was about to call you to tell you how sorry he is that you got mixed up in anything like that. We're getting together later today to go over the list of the center's volunteers."

"You don't seriously believe any of them could be involved?" Cara asked, incredulously.

"I'm taking the tack that everyone's at least potentially guilty until proven otherwise. What can you tell me about Bradley himself?"

"That he's a devoted family man and a wonderful person. You're wasting your time even considering him."

Mark shrugged. "It's my time."

"What about your job?"

"I'm on leave. That was another of the calls I made. I'll finish up at headquarters today, then that's it until this is over."

"But the case you're working on . . ."

"We cracked it last night." He gave her a sheepish grin. "I guess I didn't mention that. Anyway, I talked to James, and he'll cover anything that comes up. By the way, he's taking Diana out to dinner tonight."

"That was fast. Lord, you just reminded me, I've got to go into the office. There's a ton of stuff piled up."

"I'll drop you there," Mark said, "and pick you up this evening. If you have to go anywhere in between, ask Diana to tag along."

"Isn't that going a little too far—" Cara began.

"No," Mark broke in, unequivocally. "That creep threatened you, Cara. You have to take that seriously." A shadow passed over his lean, hard face.

"Every day in this town things happen you would not believe, and I'd just as soon keep it that way. Until I run 'Joe' to ground and put him where he belongs, you go nowhere alone."

In the face of his fierce determination, Cara could hardly disagree. Besides, she had to admit that she appreciated his protectiveness, even if it did seem a bit excessive. It was very nice, for a change, to feel that someone was taking care of her.

Still, she saw no reason to say anything to Diana who seemed to have more than enough on her mind thinking about James Muir. When, despite the crisp, clear day, Cara had lunch sent in from a nearby delicatessen, Diana barely noticed. She went about her work, alternately smiling and frowning, until at last Cara said, "We can talk about it if you think it would help?"

"About what?" Diana asked, feigning innocence.

"You know perfectly well what. How a nice, sane woman who had far too much sense to ever get involved with a cop has managed to fall for one after a single date."

"Who says I've fallen for him?"

Cara grinned at her. "You do. You might as well be wearing a sign."

"That bad, huh?"

"'Fraid so."

Diana sighed deeply. "All we did was have dinner together. He hasn't even kissed me."

"So?" Cara asked.

"It ought to take more than that. No man should be able to have such an effect with just a little conversation."

"But he has?"

"Oh, Lord, yes. Heaven help me but I absolutely cannot get that man out of my mind. Do you know, I didn't sleep a single wink last night?"

"I know the feeling," Cara murmured, glad at least that her friend had had a happier reason for being awake than she had. Gently, she added, "And I know you're worried. But isn't it better to take the risk and care about someone even if that does make you vulnerable?"

"I suppose," Diana murmured. "It's just that I got so used to being on my own, making my own decisions, not really having to take anyone else into account. Changing that will be tough."

"You know you can do it if you want to."

"Oh, I don't have any doubts about that. The thing is that about the first words out of James's mouth after we sat down to dinner were to the effect that he loved being a cop and would never give it up. I guess that constituted fair warning."

"I guess it did," Cara agreed, remembering when Mark had pretty much warned her of the same thing. "He's an honest man."

"Among other things," Diana said with a wry smile. "What it seems to come down to is that I can forget any idea of him changing jobs. Either I take him the way he is or I don't take him at all."

"Which is it going to be?" Cara asked.

"Think I know? Half of me says run like hell, the other half says this is the best thing that's come my way in a real long time, and I'd have to be an idiot to blow it."

"Personally, I've always thought you were pretty smart."

"Thanks," Diana said ruefully, "I think. Anyway, I appreciate being able to talk about it with someone who really understands. How are you and Mark doing?"

"Fine, I guess, although I'm still concerned about how well he's dealing with Rory's death. He seems to be all right, on the surface at least. It's underneath that I'm worried about."

"Has he said anything to you?"

Cara nodded. "We've talked about it, of course, but I have the feeling that we're both being very careful about what we say."

"Have you asked him to quit?"

Stung by her friend's bluntness, Cara shook her head. "No, of course not."

"Why of course? Seems to me it would be perfectly natural for you to want him out."

"I don't have the right to..."

"You love him, don't you?"

"With all my heart," Cara said softly. "But his life is still his own. He has to decide what he wants to do with it. Oh, I don't doubt," she added, "that I could use his feelings for me to get him to quit, but I won't do that."

"You're smart not to," Diana said. "Somewhere deep down inside, he'd always resent it."

"That's what I think, too, and I can't take the chance. So I have to leave it up to him, and hope for the best."

Which didn't mean that she could put the problem out of her mind. Over and over that afternoon, she wondered what Mark was doing and whether or not he was safe. At least he'd be off for a while, thanks to her own problem. A reluctant smile touched her mouth as it occurred to her that in a twisted sort of way, "Joe" might be doing her a favor.

That distasteful thought was still with her when Mark picked her up. They went back to his place for dinner and it was there, over sautéed bluefish and salad, that he dropped his bombshell.

"I'm thinking of changing jobs," he said casually, as though commenting on the weather.

Cara's eyes flew wide open. She stared at him disbelievingly. "You don't mean . . . ?"

He caught the look on her face and shook his head. "That I'd be leaving the force? No, I don't. But this opportunity came up all of a sudden, and it looks as though it might be worth my while."

"What is it?" Cara asked, fighting against the urge to get her hopes up. He wasn't talking about leaving the police altogether; she had to keep remembering that.

"When I got into work this morning," he said with a grin, "imagine my surprise to find a message saying that I was wanted in the Commissioner's office."

Cara whistled softly. "I guess that doesn't happen every day."

"It happens never. Not once in fifteen years have I had occasion to meet with the big honcho, whoever he happened to be. Anyway, I checked my tie for spots and went on over."

"What did he want?"

"He'd heard about my refusing to attend some conference one of our resident bureaucrats dreamed up."

"He called you on the carpet for something like that?" she asked incredulously.

"Not exactly. It seems the Commissioner feels that what's needed on the force is less talk and more action. He's decided to appoint an assistant commissioner to streamline the nonsense and keep everybody on their toes."

Cara sat back in her chair and stared at him. "You?"

"That's the idea."

Slowly she said, "It sounds like quite an honor."

"Oh, yeah, it is. Not to mention a promotion, raise in salary, the whole ball of wax. Plus, of course, it's a desk job. No more putting my hide on the line every day."

"I suppose you'll think about it carefully."

He shot her an enigmatic glance. "I'm not sure there really is anything to think about. It's got to be perfect from your point of view."

Cautiously, Cara said, "I'm not the one being offered the job."

"You know what I mean. Look, you've been great about not putting any pressure on me, but I know since Rory's death you have to be wishing more than ever that I'd get off the street. That's right, isn't it?"

She could hardly deny it, yet neither was she about to step into the trap he was, albeit inadvertently, laying for her. "I do worry about you," she said quietly. "That goes with the loving."

"But?"

"But that doesn't mean I think you should make sacrifices for me. I've thought about this a lot in the last few weeks, and I've come to the conclusion that hard as it is to accept, really loving someone means giving them the freedom to do what's best for themselves. Love isn't possession; it's letting go."

He studied her for a long moment, his dark eyes going back and forth over her face as though looking for the slightest sign of doubt. At length, he sighed deeply. "You really believe that."

It wasn't a question, but Cara answered it anyway. "Yes, I do. It's hardly the easiest way to live, but I think it's the best long-term."

"Long-term," he repeated slowly. "That is what we're all about, isn't it?"

She smiled faintly. "I certainly hope so."

He reached out across the table and took her hand, holding it very gently. "So do I. Wouldn't you say that's a good reason for my taking the job?"

"Sure," she agreed. "There's no question that you'd be safer behind a desk, but would you be happier?"

"Maybe. Who knows until I try?"

"If you're saying you have to do something in order to find out if it's right for you, I have to disagree. We're both at an age where we ought to know ourselves well enough to be able to make prudent judgments about what will suit us and what won't."

"Prudent," he murmured, rolling the word around on his tongue as he might an unfamiliar wine. "I've never gone in for that much. I don't mean I take unnecessary risks," he added, "but when it comes to the big things, I've always been willing to take a chance."

Cara thought of the chance he'd taken with her, and she with him. Her hand tightened on his. "Why did the Commissioner offer you this job?"

Mark laughed. "It's kind of ironic. Toward the end of every year, they figure out what percentage of his cases a detective's been able to solve. I generally do pretty well, but this time I placed first. That caught his eye so he asked around about me and decided I was what he was looking for.''

"I see what you mean by ironic," Cara murmured. "You do your job so well that he wants you to stop."

"I doubt the Commissioner would put it that way, but that is what it comes down to. Remember the Peter Principle?''

"That anyone working in an organization will eventually be promoted to his or her level of incompetence?''

"That's the one," he said with a grin. "It's a great explanation for a lot of what goes on in business, not to mention the police force.''

"But it's hardly the sort of thing you'd want to get caught up in. Not," she added, "that I think you wouldn't do the job well. In fact, I think you'd be excellent at it.''

"I'm getting conflicting messages from you," Mark said slowly. "On the one hand, you're telling me to do what's best for myself, but on the other, you seem to be hoping that I might decide the Commissioner's job was it.''

"Wishing would be a better word than hoping," Cara told him softly. "I wish you weren't on the street, I wish you were always safe, I wish I never had to worry that you'd end up like Rory. But I'm not a child, Mark. I don't expect all my wishes to come true.''

"I wish they could," he murmured, gazing down at the hand he was holding. It was slender and delicate, yet also very strong. Like her. "There's nothing I would like better than to be able to give you absolutely everything you want.''

"But if you did," she said with a smile, "what would there be for me to look forward to?"

"I can think of one or two things." He stood up, walked around the table, and held out his arms to her. She went into them without hesitation, grateful for the unfailing passion that would block out, at least for a time, the turbulence of her thoughts.

Chapter 15

By the end of that week, Cara had all but forgotten about the problem with "Joe." In retrospect, it seemed to her that she had gotten the wind up about very little. She still didn't like the idea that someone she knew had threatened her, but she was realistic enough not to be overly surprised.

"I'll change my phone number," she suggested to Mark as they were on the way home from Sunday dinner with his parents. It had been a pleasant occasion despite the tension that still lingered from the shooting. Cara privately thought that Maria and Joseph showed remarkable courage and self-restraint when they said nothing to their son about his leaving the force or made any mention of his being more careful. They clearly felt that they had no right to ask him for the former, and to dwell on the latter was completely unnecessary since Mark was hardly careless to begin with. Thinking about that, she resolved to have the same fortitude in her own situation.

"That's a good idea," Mark said, "and make sure it's unlisted. But it doesn't solve the problem. That guy is still out there and he did threaten you."

"But there's been no indication that he was serious," Cara said. "You checked with the doormen, and they haven't seen anyone suspicious hanging around. You talked with the people at the crisis center and at my office. No one aroused the least suspicion. You've checked into the possibility that there might be relatives of my father's that I don't know about who are envious of me, but no one has turned up. Not even the answering machine you put on my apartment phone has produced anything. 'Joe' hasn't called back, so we don't even have his voice on tape."

"I know what I've done," Mark said with a hint of irritation. "And I know what the results have been, or more correctly, haven't been. I've come up dry no matter which way I turn."

"You've tried every possible lead," Cara told him gently. "I couldn't have asked for better care, and I really appreciate it."

"But?"

"But nothing. That's it. I'm not holding anything back."

"Except that you think I should give it up."

"We can't go on forever worrying about 'Joe,'" she said quietly. "Sooner or later, we have to get back to normal."

"It's only been a week. That's hardly very long to investigate."

"Even when there are no further leads? You said yourself you've come up dry."

Mark sighed deeply. He had sensed this conversation was coming but had hoped to avoid it at least a little longer. She was right, of course. All the evidence pointed to "Joe" merely being a crank. There was no reason for them not to, as she said, get back to normal, except that he hated the thought of it. The ordinary pattern of his day-to-day life was simply no longer acceptable to him. He had become accustomed to her being there when he came home in the evening, being in his bed at night and across the breakfast table from him in the morning. He found that the most mundane domestic details they shared delighted him as much as the soaring ecstasy of their passion. With her, he felt settled in the best possible sense of the word.

"I don't want you to go," he said bluntly.

Cara shut her eyes for a moment, willing temptation to recede. It would be so easy to give in to him and simply go on as they were. But very little imagination was needed to see that within a short time they would be more or less officially living together. That sort of arrangement wasn't necessarily wrong for other people, but she didn't want it for herself. When the time came for her to fully share her life with a man, she wanted the commitment between them to be both clear and complete.

"I think I'd better," she murmured, not looking at him. "At least for a while."

He said nothing further until they had parked the car and were back at his apartment. In the short time she had lived there, Cara had come to feel at home among the piles of books and the comfortable furniture, far more than she did in her own more luxurious apartment. She smiled at that, thinking that compared to where she had grown up, Mark's home was luxurious. Beyond all else, it contained love.

"What's the matter?" he asked when he saw the sudden glitter of tears in her eyes.

She shook her head, turning away from him. "Nothing."

He reached out a hand. "No one cries over nothing."

"I'm just . . . being emotional."

His hand tightened, and he drew her to him. "There's nothing wrong with that."

"It can be dangerous."

A low laugh broke from him. "So can living. Don't tell me that you're going to try to suppress your emotions at this late date?"

She looked up at him, seeing the strong, clean line of jaw, his finely chiseled mouth, and the tender light in his dark eyes. "No," she whispered, "it is too late for that, isn't it?"

"Much too late," he muttered as he bent his head and took her lips.

Since the shooting, they had made love several times but always tenderly and with some care, not so much because of his wound, which had healed quickly, but for the sake of the tentative hopes flowering between them. That was forgotten as passion consumed them.

Mark's tongue plunged almost roughly into her mouth, stroking and savoring her with hard, demanding strokes. She met him fully, her nails digging into his broad shoulders, her body soft and pliant against his.

"I want you," he groaned hoarsely when he finally raised his head. "Right here, right now."

If he expected her to object, he was mistaken. Her answer was to put her hands on his shirt and rapidly begin to undo its buttons. Under other circumstances, the heat she felt radiating from him might have frightened her, but she was equally consumed by need. Her thoughts were all of his body, his strength, the beauty of his manhood. She was hardly aware of him lifting her into his arms and carrying her quickly across the living room to where a wide leather couch waited.

It had become a private joke between them, that for an apparently quite proper young lady, Cara wore blatantly sensual lingerie. With Mark's encouragement, she had banished panty hose completely from her drawers and given free rein to her love of lacy garter belts and silk stockings. She wore them with a matching pair of tiny bikini panties and the sheerest bra that didn't leave her feeling completely naked. The undergarments were costly and fragile. He made a mental note to replace the panties as they tore under his urgent hands.

"So beautiful," he gasped as he pressed her down onto the couch. Her skirt was bunched around her waist, her evening sweater slipped from her shoulders as he lifted her breasts above the cups of her bra and caressed the nipples with his thumbs.

"Mark," she moaned, "please..."

Despite the raging demands of his passion, he retained enough self-control to put her needs ahead of his own. "Please what? Tell me..."

"You...I want you...I love you...oh, no more...I can't stand..." But she could, and he saw to it that she did, until the fire burst within her and she sobbed his name. Her slender arms and legs were twined around him, her softness drawing him irresistibly, as the bonds of his restraint snapped, and he moved with breathtaking strength to possess her completely.

Cara had barely begun to descend from the pinnacle of pleasure when she was seized again and hurled upward, this time to even greater heights. The world flew away from her. She clung to Mark with all her strength, not knowing where she ended and he began. It didn't matter; two had become one and no more was needed. For an endless moment out of time they reveled in the sheer, unbridled joy of their lovemaking until, at last, passion eased and they began slowly to recover themselves.

Mark stirred first. He gazed down at her, seeing her beautiful face utterly relaxed and at peace. Overwhelming gentleness moved in him. He touched a finger lightly to her swollen mouth and murmured, "I didn't mean to be quite so... enthusiastic."

She opened her eyes and smiled at him. "It's all right."

"You aren't hurt?"

She shook her head, her smile deepening. "You could never hurt me."

A jolt of desire shot through him, stunning both in its intensity and its swift resurgence. He laughed wryly. "I might as well be eighteen again."

Cara lifted her hips and moved against him slowly and deliberately. "Is that what you were like then?"

"Not quite. After all, I didn't know you back then."

She laughed deep in her throat. "Flattery will get you... wherever it is you want to go."

"How about the bedroom?" he suggested.

"Sounds good, only one problem."

"What's that?"

"I think you melted my knees."

He nodded gravely. "Common problem."

She took a swat at him playfully. "It had better not be."

"No," he said, suddenly serious, "I've never experienced anything like this in my life. In fact, I wouldn't have even thought it was possible to feel so much."

"I know what you mean," she murmured. "It doesn't seem like the sort of thing anyone could survive."

"Maybe we didn't."

Her eyes widened, looking at him. "What does that mean?"

He shrugged, a bit abashed. "Only that when you go through something that... intense, perhaps you aren't the same person afterward."

"That's very philosophical," she said after a moment's reflection.

"That's me," he said with a grin. "A philosopher."

Cara raised her hips again, tantalizingly. "I can think of another occupation you might prefer."

"A man could die from this," he said much later as they were lying in bed together. They had finally managed to get the rest of their clothes off and were comfortably naked beneath the covers. Their bodies had long since warmed the sheets, and Cara's heart still beat wildly as she rested her head on his shoulder, one hand idly stroking the soft triangle of hair on his chest.

"There must be some way to measure it," she said idly.

He glanced down at her through eyes heavy with sated languor. "Measure what?"

"What happens between us. A voltmeter, maybe."

"We'd go right off the scale."

"Think of all the energy. If it could be harnessed..."

"Goodbye imported oil, so long nuclear reactors."

"We'd probably get a medal," she suggested.

"But where would they pin it on?"

"Ouch," she murmured, wincing. Under the sheet, her toes stroked his muscled calf until she found the precise spot where she had discovered he was ticklish.

"Cut that out," Mark gasped.

"Cut what out?"

"You know perfectly well that I'm ticklish."

"But I'm not doing anything. Oh, my toes... I'm not actually responsible for them, you know. They go their own way. Always have."

"You're crazy," he said, grinning. In their tussling, he had turned her over and now loomed above her, supporting his weight on his arms. A lock of thick ebony hair fell over his high forehead. His jaw was shadowed by a rough overlay of whiskers.

"The pot calling the kettle black," she gasped as he bent his head and rubbed his sandpapery cheeks over her achingly tender breasts.

"Crazy with love," he agreed thickly.

"Could we really die from this?" she asked still later. It was getting on close to dawn, and they had not yet slept. Instead, they had seemingly been intent on consuming each other. Their lovemaking was not without a certain variety, but far beyond the sheer mechanics of it was the emotion it both stemmed from and engendered. There seemed to be no end to their need for each other. It was born of a desperation which neither of them could ignore.

"Why do you want to leave?" Mark said at last. He lay on his back, his arms folded beneath his head, staring up at the ceiling. Beside him Cara turned slowly onto her side and propped herself up on an elbow.

"Because if I don't," she said, speaking slowly through love-bruised lips, "you're going to make a decision that may not be right for you."

"About the job?"

She nodded. "You're going to take it because of me, and I don't want that responsibility."

"We've already talked about this. I understand your feelings."

"But?"

He turned his head and studied her. "That's my line."

"I'm borrowing it. You understand my feelings, but you're still going to ignore them."

"That's not it at all. It's your feelings I'm thinking of...."

"When you make a decision that should be yours alone."

Mark sighed deeply. He didn't want to get into this again, especially since he suspected she was right. "I still say it's too soon for you to go back to your apartment."

"I'll be careful."

"Do you have any idea how many women in this city have said that?"

"It's not going to work," she told him. "If 'Joe' couldn't do it, you certainly can't."

"Do what?"

"Make me afraid."

He turned abruptly, taking hold of both her wrists and holding them trapped. "Listen to me. There is nothing wrong with some good, healthy fear."

She tried to yank her hands free, found that she could not, and glared at him. "Fear is never good, never healthy. I know."

His brows knit together. "How?"

"The whole time I was growing up, I was afraid. Afraid of my mother and her drinking. Afraid of the people who looked down on us. Afraid of myself and the anger I felt. I know what that does to you. It eats you up inside. I'm not going back to that, no matter what."

He eased his hold on her slightly, but didn't let go entirely. "What about being afraid for me?"

Her anger evaporated, leaving her weary and sad. "That I'll have to learn to live with. But no more than that. I draw the line. I refuse to let 'Joe' intimidate me."

Mark couldn't help but admire her courage. He also had to admit that she had a point. There had been no further threats, and he had turned up no evidence that "Joe," whoever he was, was a genuine danger. Yet he couldn't shake the niggling sense that he might be wrong.

Lacking any evidence of that, however, he could hardly stop her from doing what she thought best.

"There's something to be said for the old days," he grumbled, letting go of her reluctantly.

"How old?"

"Back when men were men and women were glad of it."

"I've got news for you," she said with a small laugh. "You still are, and so are we."

"What I meant was that there was a time when a man could tell his woman what to do and expect her to listen."

" 'His' woman?"

He turned to her, playfulness in his dark eyes, but beneath that an underlying hint that he was more serious than he wanted to admit. "You heard me, 'his.' An adjective indicating the possessive, as in 'mine.' "

Her hand stroked his roughened cheek tenderly, but her mouth twisted with humor. "Talk like that will get you run out of certain bars in this town."

"Quiche and salad palaces—wimp heaven."

"Not like where real men hang out?"

"No way," he murmured, nuzzling her throat. "Give me a beer, a slab of raw meat . . ."

"Raw?"

"All right, rare. A plate of onion rings, maybe throw in a chunk of cheesecake."

"Cholesterol heaven. How do you stay in such good shape?" Her hands were busy confirming that that was exactly what he was in.

"Clean thoughts."

The snort she gave might not have been very lady-like, but then Mark was of the firm opinion that bed was no place for a lady anyway. "If I weren't so tired . . ." he murmured.

"You may be but . . ." Her hand went on exploring, confirming that at least a part of him was apparently immune to fatigue.

Weariness forgotten, he turned to her, and they lost themselves in each other.

Chapter 16

"The old days," Cara murmured to herself as she looked up from the report she was supposed to be reading and stared out the windows. For mid-November, it wasn't all that bad. At least the sun was shining. For once, New York seemed in a better mood than she was herself.

"What's that you said?" Diana asked.

"What? Oh, nothing. I was just talking to myself."

"Not for the first time. You've been going around muttering to yourself all day."

"That bad?" Cara asked. "Sorry, I'll try to keep these one-sided conversations to myself."

"It's okay," Diana assured her. "Obviously, you've got something on your mind. Want to tell me about it?"

"There isn't much to tell. Mark needs to work something out for himself and until he does, we're not seeing as much of each other as we were."

"You mean about him staying on the force?"

"James told you?"

Diana nodded. "He mentioned it. That's some promotion Mark's been offered."

"Is that what James thinks?"

"Actually..." Diana broke off, apparently thinking twice about what she had been on the verge of saying.

"Let me guess," Cara said with a wry smile. "James made some remark to the effect that the brass is crazy to think that a street cop like Mark would come in from the cold."

"How did you know?"

"Because it's true, isn't it? Mark is excellent at what he does. Why should he give it up?"

"Rory Harrison's wife could come up with a reason." At the look on Cara's face, Diana said hastily, "I'm sorry, honey. That just popped out. Sometimes I've got all the tact of a steamroller."

"It's all right," Cara said wanly. "Don't think I haven't thought of it myself, more times than I can count."

"My momma always said that only a fool builds a house on quicksand."

"And nothing pulls you down quite as much as a sense of obligation, is that it? I gave up something big for you, so now you owe me."

"Plenty of couples end up on the rocky shoals of that little mistake."

"Not Mark and me," Cara said firmly. "He's going to make up his own mind, whether he wants to or not."

"Then you know what his decision is likely to be?"

Cara nodded her head. "I do, and I'll live with it . . . somehow."

"You wouldn't happen to have an extra dose of that kind of courage, would you? I sure could use it."

The two women exchanged a rueful smile before getting back to work. The remainder of the afternoon passed quickly. It was five o'clock before either of them noticed it.

"Busy tonight?" Diana asked as she and Cara were in the ladies' room combing their hair and freshening their makeup.

Cara shook her head. "Mark and I agreed we should take a breather. I'm seeing him tomorrow. You?"

"It's James's night to coach the basketball team at the Y. Say, we could take in a movie."

"I'd like to," Cara said, "but the truth is I'm dead tired. If I don't get a decent night's sleep soon, I'm afraid I'm going to collapse."

Diana laughed at her gently. "That wouldn't be the real reason why you wanted some time off from Mark, would it?"

"No, but it's definitely a bonus. There's something about that man. . . ."

"Tell me about it," Diana said wryly. "I may get old before my time, but oh, my, I'll go happy."

"Such a way for two grown-up women to talk," Cara said with a smile.

"Good for us. I never could stand the prissy, holier-than-thou type."

"Neither could I," Cara agreed. "People who have to pretend they're better than everyone else leave me stone cold."

Several women from the office down the hall came into the ladies' room then, and Diana and Cara left. "Enjoy your rest," Diana said as they left the building. She winked and hurried off toward the subway.

Cara walked home, deciding that anything was better than coping with the jam-packed buses or trying to get one of the seemingly nonexistent cabs. She enjoyed the stroll, but by the time she neared her apartment house, she had worked up quite an appetite and remembered that she had virtually nothing in her refrigerator.

That necessitated a stop at Mallone's. As usual, Mizzus was behind the cash register. She nodded to Cara as she came in. "We haven't seen you in a while, Miss."

Rather than respond to her obvious curiosity, Cara merely said, "It's a busy time, isn't it?" She glanced down at the freezer case in front of the counter and felt a sudden dart of temptation.

Normally, she managed to keep her yearning for junk food under at least some sort of control. But every once in a while, it demanded a major indulgence, especially when she happened to be unusually anxious. "I see you've gotten a shipment of gourmet ice cream," she said.

"That stuff from Vermont? Can't see what the fuss is about, myself, but the people hereabouts seem to like it."

Cara slid open the top of the case and peered more closely, still hoping that she might somehow walk away empty-handed. That didn't seem to be in the cards. "Cherry with chocolate," she murmured.

"What's that?"

"The flavor. They don't make it all the time. It's my favorite."

"Queer name for an ice cream."

Cara selected a pint, fought down the urge to take two, and slid the case closed. "That will be all," she said.

Mizzus rang up the purchase and accepted her money. Cara in turn accepted the small paper bag she was handed, wondering if she could walk down the street pretending that it contained a head of lettuce. She was about to go when she noticed a young man she hadn't seen before coming from the back of the store with several cartons to be unloaded.

Mizzus, following the direction of her glance, said, "We let Raymond go. This is Russell."

The boy smiled politely at Cara before going on about his duties.

As she headed for the door, the Mallones' son, Charles, held it open for her. "Have a nice evening, Miss Herrington."

She thanked him and went on her way.

One pint of cherry ice cream later, Cara was lying in bed, doing her best to go to sleep. Something was bothering her, but she couldn't figure out what it might be. Aside, of course, from the fact that she missed Mark terribly. She had thought that after a week of sleeping at his side, it would feel strange to be alone, but she had not expected to feel quite so forlorn. Toss and turn though she did, it was impossible for her to find a comfortable spot in a bed that seemed suddenly far too big for one person. Not only that but she was cold, and there was no one to tuck her feet up against.

"Too smart for my own good," she muttered as she punched her pillow. "Had to be noble about it and give him some time to himself. I wonder if he's asleep."

She was tempted to pick up the phone and find out, but restrained herself. If he was asleep, she would feel badly about waking him. If he wasn't, she knew perfectly well that he would suggest joining her and that she wouldn't be able to resist. And if he didn't answer at all, she would be worried sick.

"Talk about a no-win situation," she groused as she gave the phone a nasty look. In response, it rang.

Cara jumped. She stared at the phone, thinking that she must have been mistaken.

It rang again. Her hand shook slightly as she reached out to answer it.

"Cara, don't hang up."

Her first temptation was to do exactly that. At the first sound of "Joe's" voice, she had almost slammed the receiver down, but a sense of self-preservation kept her from doing so. There was a chance that she might be able to get some clue as to his identity.

"Why are you calling me again?" she asked, hating the trembling in her voice, but unable to completely conceal her fear.

"I'm still angry at you."

"There's no reason for you to be."

"Where have you been?"

Cara bit her lower lip, thinking frantically. Since he hadn't called while she was away—there hadn't even been any unexplained hang-ups recorded by her answering machine—how did he know she hadn't been at home?

"What makes you think I've been anywhere?" she asked cautiously.

"I'm not an idiot. Maybe you think I am, but you're wrong."

"I don't think that, Joe."

"Are you trying to trace this call?"

"No, of course not."

"I don't believe you. You're trying to trap me." His voice was becoming more shrill by the moment. "It won't work. I'm smarter than you think."

"I'm sure you are, Joe, but—"

"It's all your fault."

"My f—what is?"

"I couldn't concentrate, couldn't do my job."

"I don't understand."

"I'm so angry at you."

"I haven't done anything—"

"I'm going to kill you."

The phone went dead. Cara was left holding the receiver, staring at it as if the inanimate piece of plastic and wires might somehow be able to explain to her what had just happened. After a few moments, she became aware of the shrill sound of the dial tone and slowly put the receiver down. Her entire body, and even her mind itself, felt numb. A part of her seemed to be standing off to one side, saying that the whole thing was ridiculous, no one had threatened to kill her, she was having some sort of absurd dream.

Unfortunately, she knew better. A sob of pure terror broke from her throat as she reached frantically for the phone that had become both tormentor and lifeline.

Mark had always liked New York best in its predawn hours when the city came as close as it ever did to a sense of peacefulness. His particular line of work had long since taught him how deceptive that appearance could be, yet his earlier fondness lingered. There were even occasions when he deliberately got up at such an hour for the sheer pleasure of it.

This was not one of those times. As he sped along the road that cut through Central Park, he was cursing under his breath. He should have known, he should have insisted, he should have absolutely refused to let Cara return to her apartment. If he could only get his hands on that creep, he would . . .

Abruptly, he reined his thoughts in. There was nothing to be achieved by dissipating his anger in such a way. Better to contain it, let it harden and grow, so that it would be there for him when he needed it. The taut line of his mouth set even more grimly, and his dark eyes flashed with a deadly light as he pulled up in front of Cara's building, turned off the ignition and left the car double-parked.

The night doorman approached immediately, trying to wave him off. "You can't park there, buddy! You have to . . ."

Mark flashed his badge and marched past him. He punched the elevator button with his fist, then paced back and forth impatiently until the bronze doors slid open to admit him.

The ride up seemed to take forever when in fact only moments passed before he was ringing the bell at Cara's door.

"It's me," he said as soon as he heard her footsteps on the other side.

She unbolted the locks quickly and stood aside to let him in. He took one look at her white, strained face and forced himself to take a deep breath. He was all business as he said, "All right. Tell me exactly what he said."

All she had managed to get out over the phone was that "Joe" had called again and had threatened to kill her. Mark had barely heard that before he told her to make sure the door and all the windows were bolted, and he would be right over.

Now he said, "From the top, exactly."

"It was a very brief conversation," Cara murmured. She had put on her heaviest robe over her nightgown, but even so she wasn't warm. It seemed as though she might never be again. "While I was waiting for you, I wrote down everything I could remember."

She watched him as he scanned her handwritten account. All she had been able to find to write with was a pencil used for making up shopping lists. Holding it, her hand had shaken so badly that she wondered if he could decipher the words. He could, and as he did his face darkened.

"Bastard."

One word only, but the venom with which it was uttered told her a great deal about the stringent leash he was keeping on his emotions. Quietly she said, "Do you see anything there that could help?"

"Two things. First, he's somewhere in this neighborhood, someone who sees you on a regular enough basis to know when you aren't around. Second, what's this he says about his job?"

Cara peered over his shoulder at her scribblings. "About not being able to concentrate?"

Mark nodded even as he saw what little color had come back into her face drain completely away.

"Oh, my God," she murmured.

"What is it?"

"I think I know who— It can't be but..."

"Tell me."

"Raymond, at Mallone's, he was fired recently. He'd worked there since before I moved here. I used to see him two or three times a week."

"How old?" Mark demanded curtly.

"Late teens, maybe early twenties."

"Did he ever say much to you?"

Cara shook her head. "No, just hello, have a nice day, that sort of thing. He was always very polite."

"Do you have any idea where he lives?"

"None at all, but the Mallones should have an address." She glanced at the clock on the living-room mantel. "They'll be opening up in a couple of hours."

"I'll be waiting for them. In the meantime, let's get you back into bed."

"I can't possibly sleep."

"We'll see. I'll fix you some warm milk." The face she made wrung a smile from him. "Okay, how about brandy instead?"

"Honestly, I don't think I could keep it down." She leaned against him, her arms around his waist. "Just hold me."

He did that, and more. After he had carried her to bed, he lay beside her, holding her cradled in his arms and gently stroked her hair until, at last, as the sky was lightening, she drifted off to sleep. Only when he was certain that she wouldn't wake up did he gently disengage himself.

On his way through the living room, he paused and jotted a note down on the back of the paper she had used to record the conversation. "Gone to Mallone's for address, then after Raymond. Stay put. Alarm on."

He left the note where she would be sure to see it if she awoke. As he let himself out, he carefully turned the burglar alarm on and locked the door behind him.

Mr. Mallone was reaching in his pocket for the key to open the store when Mark approached him. He had been waiting near the corner and had noticed the Cadillac pull up. The tall, beefy man who got out looked like the type who would begrudge someone the time of day. Mark moved quickly to give him no choice but cooperation.

"Police," he said, showing his badge. "I want some information."

"What's this all about?" Mallone asked, trying to look unconcerned, but not succeeding very well. He had the typical expression of strained innocence common to those who nurture a niggling sense of guilt. "We haven't had any trouble here."

"And I'm sure you don't want any. You had a young man working for you, Raymond someone or other. I want whatever you've got on him."

By this time, Mallone had gotten the door open. They stepped inside, where he switched on the lights and automatically glanced around, assuring himself that his domain was still intact. Mark gave him a few seconds, then said, "Now."

Mallone's attention snapped back. He shook his head. "Raymond doesn't work here anymore. I fired him." He smiled slightly, undoubtedly congratulating himself for having had the foresight to get rid of someone who attracted the notice of the police. Then came the usual prurient curiosity to know the unsavory details. "What's he done, anyway?"

Rather than answer him, Mark said, "You must have records—social security, IRS, that sort of thing. His address would be on them."

"Records...sure, sure. We're scrupulous about that sort of thing. I always say to the Mizzus, cheating the government is just like cheating ourselves."

"Right," Mark said, making no pretense of believing him. "I'll wait while you dig it out."

Realizing that no further information would be forthcoming, Mallone reluctantly led him to the back of the store where a small, dimly lit cubicle served as an office. From a battered metal desk, he drew an equally disreputable-looking file box. He licked his thumb and forefinger before riffling through the cards it held.

After a moment, he pulled one out and handed it to Mark. "Here it is. I can't let you take that, of course, but you can copy down the..."

"Thanks," Mark said, tossing it back to him. He had already memorized the particulars he needed. From the pocket of his slacks, he withdrew a small card which he gave to Mallone. "If Raymond shows up here, call this number. Ask for Lieutenant James Muir. He'll know what it's about."

"Sure, sure, but what..."

Mark was gone before the words were out.

Raymond Diaz lived uptown on 125th Street. It was a rough neighborhood, but no rougher than many others Mark had coped with. He felt no hesitation as he parked his car, left the police I.D. clearly visible behind the windshield, and walked toward the building Raymond had given as his residence. There was a chance some of the kids already hanging around on the street would take it into their heads to trash the car as a way of expressing their contempt for the police, but there was an even bigger chance of their doing it if he let them think he was a civilian. At any rate, he had far too much on his mind to worry about that.

The six-story red brick apartment house had been built half a century before and still retained a few remnants of what had once been a more gracious existence. They were all but obscured by the scrawled graffiti on the walls and the various smells permeating the stale air.

The front door lacked both lock and knob; it was propped open. The tenant listing was on a metal plate that had been half ripped out of the wall. It hung by the wires that were supposed to activate the bell system to each apartment, but which had long since ceased to function. Beside one of the bells Mark found the name "R. Diaz."

The elevator was out of order. He took the steps to the fifth floor two at a time and was barely out of breath when he reached the top. All his attention was focused on his quarry. He slid his right hand underneath his jacket as with his left he knocked on the apartment door.

Chapter 17

There was a sound of movement inside, then a woman's voice said softly, *"¿Quién es?"*

"Police, open up."

He heard a soft gasp, followed by fumbling with the locks. A young, delicately built Hispanic woman opened the door. She was looking at him with wide, dark eyes and a very apprehensive expression. "Please," she said in softly accented English, "what do you want?"

"Raymond Diaz, is he here?"

"What's going on?" A young man came out of the other room. He was taller than the woman, slender but muscular. Mark put his age at about twenty. He seemed to have interrupted the man in the process of getting dressed. He was buttoning a blue workshirt as he came toward them. "Who are you, man?"

"Police," Mark said again. He took out his identification and showed it to them both. "Are you Raymond Diaz?"

The young man nodded. "That's right." He looked suspiciously at Mark and studied his I.D. carefully. "Sabatini, homicide. Are you investigating something?"

"You could say that. I'm here about Cara Herrington."

The young man's eyebrows shot up. He looked instantly concerned. "Miss Herrington? What happened to her?"

Mark frowned. Either the guy was an incredibly good actor or he really had no idea what was going on. Not only that, but he seemed genuinely worried about Cara. "Nothing yet," he said finally. "Were you fired recently from Mallone's Grocery?"

Raymond nodded slowly. The young woman cast him a worried, fearful glance. In the next room, a baby began to cry. Raymond gave the girl a reassuring smile. "Go to Pablo. It will be all right."

She looked unconvinced, but did as he said. When she had left, Raymond said, "Mallone fired me. So what?"

"Why?"

"Ask him."

Mark took a step closer. He was on very thin ice and knew it, but the thought of Cara in danger drove him on. "No games, Diaz. Straight talk only. Got it?"

"Hey, man, you burst into my apartment, scaring my wife and asking me strange questions. You've got no warrant, no explanation, nothing. What makes you think you can get away with that?"

"My sincere conviction that you don't want any more trouble than you can handle."

Raymond thought about that for a moment, and about the cold light in Mark's eyes. Then he exhaled softly. "All right, no trouble. Mallone fired me because he thought I was stealing."

"Were you?"

He shook his head vehemently. "No way, man. I've got a wife and a kid. You think I'm going to take the chance of getting sent to jail and leaving them on their own?"

"Maybe you needed the money."

"I've got money, man. I work." He drew himself up proudly and glared at Mark. "I walked straight out of Mallone's and into another job, a better one. And you know why? Because I don't go in for any funny stuff. I play straight."

"Then how come Mallone thought you were stealing?"

Raymond shrugged. "He's not too crazy about people whose skin is darker than his, so when stuff turned up missing, I was the easiest to blame."

"What kind of stuff?"

"Grocery stock, cartons of gourmet food items, sides of beef, that kind of thing."

"Substantial?"

"Couple of thousand the first time, more when it kept happening."

Mark's eyebrows rose. "That's a lot of money. If you weren't doing it, who was?"

Raymond hesitated. He looked at Mark carefully, as though assessing the chances of him believing what he had to say. Finally, he said, "You look like you've been around a while. You've got to know as well as I do why most people steal in this town.''

Mark did; New York's drug problem was by no means unique, but it was responsible for a great deal of the crime that went on. His stomach muscles knotted. ''Give me a name, Raymond.''

This time the young man did not hesitate. ''It's the Mallones' son, Charles. He's a little cracked. You know what I mean?''

Mark was very much afraid that he did. ''How little?''

''Enough to still function, but that's about it. Underneath, he's as crazy as everyone on that stuff gets. I don't think his parents have a clue as to what's going on, mainly because they don't want to know.''

''I need to use your phone,'' Mark said. He punched in Cara's number rapidly, then cursed as he heard a busy signal.

''Thanks for the help,'' Mark said as he put down the receiver. He was out the door before Raymond could blink. Moments later, he was on the street, heading toward his car.

Cara had woken up shortly after Mark left. She turned over in the bed, muzzy with sleep, and tried to remember why she was feeling apprehensive. Recollection flooded back, jerking her upright. She looked around, hoping to see Mark. When she did not, she got out of the bed and went in search of him, but found only his note.

Knowing that she was alone in the apartment didn't exactly make her feel comfortable, but it wasn't a major problem either. The small red light of the burglar alarm was on, reassuring her that no one could enter without her being aware of it. A glance at the windows confirmed that they were still securely locked. So long as she stayed where she was, she couldn't see what harm could possibly befall her.

Except that she was ravenously hungry. The plain fact was that however many zillions of calories might be in a pint of super rich ice cream, it hardly made a meal. Her stomach growled as she walked into the kitchen and glanced in the refrigerator.

If she discounted a suspiciously old carton of sour cream and a six-pack of beer, it was empty. The cupboards weren't much better. Try though she did, she couldn't stand the idea of potato chips that early in the morning, especially not in the absence of dip to go with them.

Cara sighed resignedly and headed for the phone. Fortunately, Mallone's delivered.

Mark pressed his foot to the accelerator and swerved to change lanes, cutting directly in front of another car. The irate driver blasted his horn, but Mark ignored him. He had no thought except to get to Cara's as quickly as possible.

Even at that early hour, traffic was heavy, but it was also moving steadily for a change. He glanced at his watch and calculated that he could be at Cara's apartment within twenty minutes. Provided nothing happened to delay him.

He left the FDR Drive at 75th Street and turned east. He was within half a dozen blocks of his objective when traffic suddenly ground to a halt. Mark cursed and slammed his fist against the steering wheel. He rolled down the window and looked out. Up ahead, at the next intersection, a truck and a taxi had collided. Both drivers were out on the street, waving their arms and screaming at each other.

His language worsening by the moment, he reached for the radio transmitter below his steering wheel. When the dispatcher answered, he said, "Sabatini, homicide. I need a call patched through fast." Quickly, he gave Cara's number, then waited as the well-trained operator set about putting it through. A moment later he again heard a busy signal.

"Damn."

"Want me to try again?" the dispatcher asked.

"No, put me through to headquarters."

The officer who picked up there must have realized instantly from Mark's voice that there was trouble. He listened silently as the problem was outlined for him, then said, "Let me make sure I've got this straight. We've got a possible victim unavailable by phone and a possible perpetrator somewhere nearby?"

"That's it. I want a prowl car at Miss Herrington's building pronto, also another to pick up Mallone." Quickly, he gave them both addresses. "He can't be allowed to get anywhere near her."

"I'll take care of it immediately," the officer assured him. "What's your status?"

"Stuck in traffic," Mark said with disgust. Up ahead, he could still see the two drivers arguing. A policeman had arrived on the scene and was attempting to calm them down, but it would clearly be several minutes at least before the intersection was cleared. "But I'm about to fix that," he muttered.

The palm of his hand struck the horn and stayed there as he maneuvered his car out of the line of traffic and over toward the sidewalk. There was a gap at the curb near a fire hydrant. He pulled in there and jumped out.

The policeman, glancing in his direction, yelled at him and tried to wave him back. Mark ignored him. He slammed the car door and started running.

Cara had tried Mallone's twice before getting through to the store. When she finally did, Mizzus answered the phone. "I need a few things," Cara said, "and I'd like to have them delivered."

"That's a bit difficult," Mizzus told her.

Cara had hardly expected her to say otherwise; Mizzus would go to her grave before cheerfully agreeing to do anything. In her starchiest tone, she said, "I'm sure you can manage." Quickly, she reeled off half a dozen simple items which not even Mizzus could claim were unavailable.

"I'd appreciate it if Russell could bring them over now," Cara said when she had finished.

"Russell isn't in today; he called in sick. Just started the job and already he's slacking off. You can't count on anyone these days. Why I tell you it's a crying shame the way people—"

"Charles, then," Cara said, cutting off Mizzus' diatribe. "Is he available?"

"Just a moment, I'll see." There was the murmur of conversation on the other end of the phone before Mizzus said with some surprise, "He's putting the order together. He says he'll be right over."

"Good, I'll tell the doorman to let him up."

While she waited, she went back into the bedroom and got dressed. She had to reach far back in her closet to find the jeans and bulky old turtleneck that were what she thought of as her "comfort clothes." There was a fireplace in the living room that actually worked. She found a paraffin log and placed it carefully on the rack under the open flue. Within minutes, she had a cheerful blaze going.

As she got up and dusted her hands off, the doorbell rang. She hurried to answer it, remembering as she did so to switch off the burglar alarm. Charles smiled at her as she opened the door.

"Morning, Miss Herrington," he said as he stepped inside. "I've got all your stuff here. Hope you're feeling all right?"

"I'm fine," she assured him as she relocked the door and, feeling a bit silly even as she did so, switched the alarm back on. "My wallet's in the kitchen. If you'd..."

He followed her in there, setting the bag down on the counter. As she rummaged in her purse, she became aware of him studying her. When she had collected the money and turned to give it to him, he merely smiled again. "You don't have to do that, Miss Herrington."

"Pardon?"

"Pay for the groceries. It isn't necessary."

Bewildered, she shook her head. "That's very nice of you, Charles, but I don't think your parents would approve."

His small eyes narrowed beneath his lank brown hair. "They don't approve of anything I do anyway, so who cares."

His eyes darted back and forth as he spoke. He was clearly nervous. Cara wondered why, even as she felt a mild surge of irritation at having to put up with his adolescent temperament when she had more than enough problems of her own.

"That's too bad, Charles, but you'll have to take the money." She held it out to him firmly, but he continued to ignore it. Instead, he stared at her, his eyes raking her up and down.

"You're really beautiful, you know that? Even in those old clothes, you look like a million dollars." He laughed shrilly. "But then that's what you are, isn't it? A million dollars, maybe more."

Cara had run out of patience. Moreover, she was becoming distinctly nervous at the tack their conversation was taking. Resolutely, she said, "Thanks for bringing the groceries over, Charles. I have to get to work now, so—"

"You're lying."

Her mouth dropped open. She thought she must have heard him wrong. "What did you say?"

"You're lying. You'd never go to work dressed that way. You're not planning on going anywhere."

"Whether I am or not is my business, Charles. You have to leave now."

Instead of obeying, he merely shrugged and said, "Don't call me that."

"What . . . ?"

"Charles. I hate that name." His thin mouth twisted in a smile. "Call me Joe."

"Oh, God. . . ." Cara took a step backward, only to run up against the kitchen wall. Frantic thoughts darted through her mind. She had never even considered that Charles Mallone might be "Joe," so utterly innocuous had he always seemed to her. But now, with the painful benefit of hindsight, she recognized the familiar quality in his voice that had registered with her even when he attempted to muffle it. And she realized something else as well: that the main reason she

had never paid much attention to Charles was that he had always instinctively turned her off. She had been faintly repelled by him all along without even realizing it.

"I tricked you, didn't I?" he said as he walked toward her, closing the small distance between them. "I made you think it was Raymond."

"Yes," Cara murmured, though her throat was so tight she could barely speak, "you did."

"You should have been nicer to me."

"I-I'm sorry...."

"It's too late," he said calmly, all the while continuing to smile at her in a cold, inhuman way that chilled her to the core. "I wanted you to like me, but you hung up on me instead. Now I'm going to hang up on you." He laughed and, when she failed to join in, said, "That's a joke. Don't you get it?"

Fighting the sickness rising within her, Cara shook her head. "No, I don't."

"Hang up, cut off, stop. I told you on the phone what I'm going to do."

Cara heard him, but only dimly. She had known from the moment he revealed himself what he intended to do; hearing it again added only marginally to her rampant fear. Not for a moment did she doubt that he meant exactly what he said.

Frantically measuring the distance between them, she wondered if there was any way she could get to the front door. Desperate as she was to believe that she might have a chance, she realized it wasn't so. Charles was tall, with long arms and legs. She would barely reach the kitchen door before he would be on her.

The thought of him touching her made her skin crawl. She rubbed her arms through the bulky sweater while she fought to remain calm. There was a set of kitchen knives in a wooden holder on the counter. Charles's gaze shifted to them. He closed in on her, standing so close that she could smell the sourness of his breath.

"First, you're going to show me where everything is."

"Every—?"

"The jewels, the money. I have to have them."

"But I don't—"

"Stop lying."

"I'm not . . ."

He grabbed her arm and twisted it behind her. With his other hand he reached for the largest of the knives. "Why do you have to be so stubborn? This is all your fault to begin with, and now you're making it worse. I'm really getting annoyed with you."

Still gripping her arm, he pushed her out of the kitchen and through the living room. "I'll bet you keep everything in the bedroom. That's what women always do."

"I swear, I'm telling you the truth. . . ."

He jerked on her arm hard, and a bolt of pain shot through her, making her cry out. "Shut up! You're trying to make me do this too fast, but I won't let you get away with it. We're going to do it my way."

"All right," Cara cried. She was all but overwhelmed by sheer, blinding rage that urged her to kick out at him however she could. But she knew how completely futile—and dangerous—that would be. "I'll do whatever you want, only please, stop hurting me."

Gratified by what he took to be her submission, Charles eased his hold on her slightly, but kept pushing her toward the bedroom. Cara stumbled and would have fallen if he hadn't jerked her upright.

When they reached the bedroom, he let go of her and pushed her hard in the direction of the dresser. "Get the stuff."

"I told you, I don't—"

She broke off, gasping as he brandished the knife. *"Get it."*

Numbly, all but crushed by the full weight of her terror, she whispered, "I don't have any jewels. I don't bother with them. And I don't keep a lot of cash in the apartment. All I have is what's in my wallet."

He was silent for a moment, as though considering what she had said. She had just begun to hope that he might actually believe her, when he shook his head. "You're lying again. That's all you do. Lie, lie, lie." With each repetition, he stabbed the air with the knife.

He stared at her, then abruptly nodded, having come to some decision. "All right. We'll do it your way. I'll find the stuff later."

He raised the knife and took a step toward her.

Cara screamed. She ducked under his arm and ran, no longer thinking about whether or not she had any chance of getting away. A desperate gamble was better than none at all, given the alternatives facing her. She managed to reach the living room, but he caught her there, knocking her to the floor and falling with her. The knife dropped onto the carpet some little distance from them as they rolled toward the fireplace.

Charles's hands were on her throat, squeezing hard. She couldn't breathe, and colored lights whirled before her eyes. Her lungs were on fire as she tried desperately to break his grip.

Above her, his face distorted with rage, he chanted over and over, "Kill you, kill you."

The blackness was closing in from all directions, and her vision narrowed down to small points of light. Cara's hand fumbled across the stone in front of the fireplace until it struck cold metal. Her fingers curled around the poker's iron shaft. With the last of her strength, she lifted it.

Chapter 18

Cara watched in disbelief as Charles, reeling from the blow she had struck him, still managed to get to his knees. Blood was oozing from the side of his head, where the poker had hit him, but he seemed unaware of his injury.

The shock to her own body from near-strangulation had made it impossible for her to do more than crawl a few yards away from him. The poker lay where she had dropped it near the fireplace, and the knife was still beyond her reach. But not beyond his. As he staggered to his feet, he looked at her and laughed.

"You can't hurt me. I'm Superman. I'm the strongest man there is. I can do anything and no one can stop me." He laughed again, insanely, and picked up the knife.

"Now," he said as he came toward her, "I'm going to make you very, very sorry."

Cara closed her eyes. She had no strength left. Her lips moved in a silent prayer. She was filled with a regret so profound that it even swamped her fear. The cold steel touched her throat. If only she and Mark had had more time together. . . .

The sound of glass shattering filled the room. At the same time the heavy front door was smashed in, and the burglar alarm went off.

"Police. Freeze!"

Charles looked up, saw the uniformed men coming toward him from the doorway, and turned to run. Mark stood in front of the window he had broken through and watched him come. Mark's gun was drawn, held unshakably in both hands, his feet planted apart in the shooter's stance. He had an absolutely clear line of fire; there was no way he could possibly miss.

"No," Cara screamed, *"don't."*

He hesitated a fraction of a second, long enough for the other policemen to reach Charles and wrestle him to the ground. As the young man's hands were cuffed behind his back and he was hauled to his feet, Mark slowly slid his gun back into its shoulder holster. He swallowed hard and took a deep breath before he crossed the room to where Cara lay.

His hands on her were very gentle and very careful as he automatically searched for signs of injury. His normally burnished skin had a gray cast and a jagged pulse beat in the hollow of his cheek. She touched a finger to it gently. "I'm all right. Really."

"You're bruised," he said hoarsely.

"It's nothing. He didn't have a chance to do more. You came in time." Holding on to him, she got to her feet. The powerful muscles of his upper arms were bunched so tightly that they must have been painful. Gently, she smiled at him. "It's over, Mark, truly."

He glanced away from her to Charles, who was being led toward the door. In the aftermath of his capture, the young man seemed to have almost visibly deflated. The maniacal light was gone from his eyes, and his head drooped wearily.

Gruffly, Mark said, "You'd better take him to detox."

One of the policemen nodded. "He's crashing fast."

"Drugs," Cara murmured when they were gone. "I should have known. He was so crazed...so completely out of touch with reality...and he had such unbelievable strength."

"That all goes with what he was putting into his body. He's cooked his brain and no matter what they do for him in detox, he's going to have a hell of a time putting it back into shape. But then," he added remorselessly, "he'll have plenty of time to try."

Cara managed a wan smile. "No plea bargaining on this one?"

"Not a chance. Between your testimony and mine, not to mention what the other officers saw when they came in here, old Charles is going away for a good, long stretch."

One of the other officers, who had overheard what Mark said, looked at them and shrugged. "He may never come out. A lot of these guys don't. They cut their life expectancies tremendously with that stuff."

"Too bad," Mark said bluntly. Charles had been led stumblingly from the apartment. A cold wind blew in through the shattered living-room window, making the front door with its shot-out lock bang back and forth.

"You can't stay here," he said to Cara. He turned to the officer in charge. "Any reason why she can't give her statement tomorrow at the precinct?"

The man shook his head. "None that I can think of. Bring her round in the morning, and we'll take care of it."

Mark nodded and took Cara's arm. "Let's go. They'll take care of the door and window. We can come back tomorrow and pick up your things."

Under other circumstances, his peremptoriness might have irked her, but not then. She still had the image of him coming through the window firmly implanted in her mind. He had risked his life to save her. The thought of what might have happened, not to her but to him, made her tremble.

Neither of them spoke as they left her building and walked back to where he had left his car. He had wanted her to wait while he got it, but she had refused. The mere idea of being alone dismayed her, yet she also realized that had she been with anyone other than Mark, she would still have been terrified.

As they drove to his place, she leaned her head back and shut her eyes. Silence lengthened between them until they reached his apartment. Only then did she look at him and say, "I hope that you don't make a habit of flying through the air like that."

"First time," he assured her as he locked the door behind them.

"You could have been badly hurt," she murmured, "from the broken glass, not to mention if you'd fallen...."

"I could have been... Do you have any idea how ridiculous that sounds? You were the one in danger. That lunatic..."

"Didn't you think of your own safety at all?" she interrupted softly.

"I hate to disappoint you, but I most certainly did. I was securely roped and I was wearing a bulletproof vest. Maybe that doesn't sound very romantic, but—"

"Actually, it sounds extremely romantic."

"I'm not apologizing. It wouldn't have done you any good if I'd blown it— What did you say?"

"Romantic. You, me. Life in general." She was smiling broadly now, almost laughing with the giddiness of sheer relief, the effects of which went far beyond the events of the past few hours. Slowly she was beginning to realize that she had confronted something more than a sad, damaged young man. She had come face-to-face with all her fears for Mark and was well into the process of coming to terms with them.

"Remember what I said about not wanting to pressure you into taking that desk job?" she asked.

"Of course I do. That was very selfless, very generous."

"I lied."

"What?"

"You heard me. Deep down inside I thought that if I refused to take the responsibility, you'd have to. And knowing that you love me, I figured there was a good chance you'd feel obligated to spare me any chance of ending up like Linda Harrison."

"You won't end up like her," Mark said flatly. "Whatever I have to do, I'll make sure of that."

"You'll go live in a cave somewhere, drink purified water and breathe filtered air? Never take the slightest risk of something happening to you?"

"No, of course not, that's unrealistic. But I can get off the street. I'll call the Commissioner tomorrow."

"And possibly get hit by a truck the next day. Or, far more likely, live with the stress of being something you aren't until it finally destroys you. Do you really think Linda would have wanted to see her husband becoming less and less himself as the years went by, to have watched him shrivel up in front of her until he was no different from the mass of dissatisfied, discontented people who have failed to be true to themselves?"

"No, of course not," Mark murmured. "Linda loved Rory far too much for that."

"And I love you too much. You, Mark Sabatini, homicide detective, street cop. The man who flies through windows, who puts his life on the line, but who thinks twice before taking someone else's. You know," she added, "if you hadn't been there today, Charles would probably have gone out that window, at the very least."

He raised his eyebrows. "Do you care?"

"Yes, as a matter of fact, I do. Oh, I'm not denying I want to see him punished to the full extent of the law. But I also hope that other policeman was wrong and that he does somehow recover."

"You must know that the odds of that are very small."

"Maybe, but they beat the odds of recovering from a twenty-three story fall. It's no exaggeration to say that you saved his life as well as mine. What's more, you saved his twice." She asked quietly, "Why didn't you shoot him?"

Mark hesitated. It would have been the easiest thing in the world to say that he had held off firing at Mallone because she had asked him to. But the simple fact of the matter was that such decisions were made at a gut level, and in such a short period of time, that nothing she could have said or done would have made any difference. He hadn't shot the kid because he hadn't wanted to.

Softly, he said, "I told you about the one time I shot someone."

"And how much you've always regretted it, even though in that case you had absolutely no alternative. But this time there was, and you took it. I'm glad, just as I'm glad that you took the precautions you did. You're not out to prove how tough you are, and that more than anything is my best assurance that you'll stay alive."

He nodded. They looked at each other for a long moment. When he opened his arms, silently calling to her, she went to him unhindered by the slightest shadow of doubt.

"You know," she said as he held her tenderly, "I've always liked this apartment better than my own."

"How come?"

"It's a home, not a stage set."

He laughed gently. "Your place isn't that bad, though I have to admit I wouldn't exactly relish the idea of living there."

"Then what do you say," she murmured as she touched petal-soft kisses to the nape of his neck, "to my doing the other owners a favor and selling the place?"

He took a step back so that he could look at her. "You really wouldn't mind?"

She shook her head. "On the contrary, it would be a relief. I've decided I'm not really cut out to be a rich girl."

"You are in the only ways that count," he said gently, drawing her back against him. The slender strength of her reassured him tremendously. He could feel the steady beat of her heart against his chest and the smooth warmth of her skin through the bulky sweater. He closed his eyes for a moment and gave silent thanks to be holding the only riches he would ever want.

When he looked at her again, his eyes were alight with a fire she was only too happy to recognize. "About these clothes..."

"Great, aren't they? Absolutely the latest style."

"That's nice." He slid his hands under the sweater, stroking the silken line of her back and was gratified to feel her tremble. "But it looks awfully hot, and I wouldn't want you to get prickly heat."

"Terrible stuff," she agreed as he slipped the sweater over her head and let it drop on the floor. Her bra went next, and she stood before him naked from the waist up, her hair tumbling around her shoulders, and a purely female smile lifting the corners of her mouth.

"You take my breath away," he murmured hoarsely.

Her pride at being able to move him like that brought a flush of color to her cheeks. Feeling very daring, she kicked off her shoes, then slowly unsnapped the jeans and slid the zipper down. Holding his eyes with her own, she stepped out of them.

He took a deep, harsh breath. The exquisite lingerie he had become accustomed to seeing was missing.

Instead, she wore a pair of utilitarian cotton panties and, as her only other remaining apparel, gym socks. His dark gaze danced mischievously as his eyes raked up and down the slender length of her body. "I should have warned you about this thing I have for gym socks."

"Do you really?"

"They drive me absolutely wild. It must be some leftover adolescent fetish, but I cannot be trusted anywhere near gym socks. Especially not old ones."

She lifted one foot and regarded it fondly. "These have been around awhile."

"That only adds to their allure. First," he continued as he walked toward her, "I'm going to do the swashbuckling bit and carry you into the bedroom. Then I'm going to peel each of those sinfully seductive socks off your gorgeous feet. Then I'm going to take off..."

"I get the message," Cara said. Her flush was spreading down her throat and over the crests of her bare breasts. She could hardly breathe, and didn't mind in the least. Any such mundane consideration was completely beyond her. Nothing mattered except Mark, being there with him, looking ahead to all they would share.

"And then," he went on relentlessly, "I'm going to taste every inch of you until you're screaming with the pleasure of it."

Mark Sabatini—homicide detective, street cop, human being—was above all a man of his word.

Epilogue

A little more chicken," Maria suggested, offering the platter to Cara. "And take another piece of bread. You don't want to waste the sauce."

Mark smothered a laugh and gave his wife an encouraging look. "Have some more salad, too, sweetheart. It's good for the baby."

"I don't mind if I do," Cara said, helping herself to generous portions. "Since the morning sickness stopped, I seem to be starved all the time."

"That's a good sign," Joseph said from his seat at the head of the table. "Maybe it's twins."

His son shot him a startled look, prompting Joseph to grin. "What did I say? Twins would be great, wouldn't they?"

"Oh, yeah," Mark murmured, "sure. But seriously, the doctor says there's only one."

"There's plenty of time for more," Maria advised. "You've only been married a couple of years. What's the rush?"

Cara and Mark exchanged a startled glance. Ever since their wedding, Maria had been discreetly hinting about her desire for more grandchildren. She'd been very nice about it, but no one had been left in any doubt of how she felt.

"You'll have this one," Maria went on, serenely ignoring their surprise, "you'll get a little experience...you'll realize your apartment is too small...."

"And we'll buy that house down the street," Mark finished for her. He reached across the table and gave her a hug, laughing as she tried to swat him away. "You don't fool anyone, Mama. You've got it all figured out and you're just waiting for us to realize it."

"And what's the harm?" she inquired sedately. "This is a nice neighborhood, good schools, not to mention an excellent investment. You could do a lot worse."

"Seriously," Joseph said, "you should think about it. There's a great deal to be said for families living near each other."

"I agree with you," Cara said. She meant it from the bottom of her heart. The Sabatinis had welcomed her without reservation. From the moment she and Mark had announced their intention to wed, she had been treated as a full-fledged member of the family. Despite the difference in their ages, she and Maria had become good friends. Mother-in-law jokes were lost on Cara, who had nothing in her life to relate them to.

She gave her husband a gently chiding look. "Don't you think you should tell them?"

"All right," he said with a laugh. "Cara and I looked at the house this afternoon on the way over here. We both think it's got real possibilities."

"And..." his mother urged.

"And we bought it. There, are you satisfied?"

Maria exclaimed with delight, "That's wonderful news."

"It certainly is," Joseph added. "We were concerned you might think it was too big a place for you."

"Not really," Mark said. "After all, the six kids will take a lot of room...."

"Don't listen to him," Cara advised. "That's still in negotiation."

"Seriously," Mark explained, "we need a place that size because we're going to have to do a lot more entertaining."

"Entertaining for what?" Joseph asked.

"The foundation," Maria suggested. "All the projects Cara supports. People like to be wined and dined."

"I could never compete with Muffy Ste. Martin," Cara said. Maria and Joseph had accompanied them to one of Muffy's parties. For weeks afterward, Maria had referred to her as "that woman," and Joseph had merely rolled his eyes.

"Actually," Mark said, "the entertaining is because of me. I'm changing jobs."

Maria and Joseph went very still. They exchanged a look that drove home to Cara, watching them, how long they had waited for this moment. Mark understood it, too. He put a hand over his wife's as he said, "I've had two more years on the street than I figured to have. Cara's backed me all the way, even though there have been times when it was rough on her. But

I'm satisfied now that I've done everything in that area that I can. Even if we didn't have a baby coming it would be time to move on."

"James is getting out, too," Cara said. The Sabatinis knew Diana and James; they had attended their wedding a few months before.

"I'm glad," Maria said simply. "It's a loss to the force, but better that than you should go on too long."

"Not a total loss," Mark said. "We're going to be a working liaison between the department and community organizations. The idea is to get clearer lines of communication going and see what can be done about giving the guys on the street more support."

"That sounds like it won't be any easier than what you've been doing," Joseph ventured. "Plenty of people are too suspicious of the police to be in any hurry to cooperate with them."

"Unfortunately, you're right. But we have to start somewhere. This city belongs to the people. Certain elements tend to forget that. It's time they were reminded."

"He said that to Philip Bradley," Cara said with a laugh, "the head of the crisis center, the other night at a party, and can you guess what Philip told him?"

Maria and Joseph shook their heads.

"That it would make a great campaign slogan. Philip's very involved in city politics. He's trying to get Mark interested, too."

"I vote," Mark said. "That's the extent of my interest."

"Gracie Mansion is such a nice house," Maria murmured. "A mayor with a big family would be very comfortable there."

Mark rolled his eyes. "Please, Mama, it wasn't enough I tracked down killers? You want me to deal with politicians, too?"

"I won't say another word," Maria said, and kept her promise. However, just so he wouldn't think he could boss her around, she got out Mark's baby pictures after dinner and insisted on showing them to Cara, who laughed so hard that her sides were still hurting hours later as they lay side by side in bed.

"I want you to give me your solemn word," Mark said, "that you will never do that to our child."

"Why not? You were so cute. Those huge dark eyes and that wonderful curly hair. Come to think of it, you still have all that." Her hand slid down his bare chest to touch him lingeringly. "Not to mention a great deal more."

"Quit trying to distract me."

"Is that what I'm doing?"

"Yes, and you're very good at it."

"Oh, I'm sorry, I'll stop."

He took her hand and firmly replaced it where it had been so pleasantly occupied. "This is no time to turn agreeable."

She gave him one of her best raised-eyebrows looks. "Surely, you aren't suggesting that I'm usually difficult?"

He turned on his side and gazed at her with all the deep love his passionate nature was capable of stamped on his rugged features. "Difficult... complicated... fascinating... tantalizing... If I live to be a hundred, I'll never get over the fact that we were lucky enough to find each other."

She snuggled against him, her fingers tracing the soft triangle of hair across his broad chest. "Only a hundred? What happens after that?"

"We'll work on it," he murmured as he touched his mouth to hers. Since learning of the baby, his lovemaking had been achingly tender. He took exquisite care with her, which raised her to such a peak of anticipation that she feared she wouldn't be able to survive it. It seemed only fair that she return the favor.

Afterward, as she lay with her head on his shoulder, she murmured sleepily, "Any regrets?"

His hand that had been tenderly stroking her back stilled. He loved her too much to be less than honest. Silently, he reached into himself, searching for the truth. Would he miss the excitement, the challenge, the pride of being on the street? Certainly, that was what had kept him there as long as it had. But life was change; she had taught him that.

It was also—for those fortunate enough—love. He smiled in the gentle darkness and gathered her closer. "About those second hundred years . . ."

* * * * *

*...and now an exciting short story
from Silhouette Books.*

*

HEATHER GRAHAM POZZESSERE

Shadows on the Nile

CHAPTER 4

Jillian had no idea how long the car careened through the twisting streets of Cairo. She was nearly unconscious by the time that it stopped; the exhaust fumes had penetrated to the trunk, and she felt cramped and nauseated.

She tried desperately to free herself from the blanket, but she accomplished nothing. Then rough hands dragged her from the car. She was carried—wriggling and screaming—for an unknown distance, and then things became worse. She was slung over the back of a creature that she identified by its scent and sound as a camel, and her misery grew. She could barely breathe, and every awkward step of the camel slammed into her anew. Once again she had no concept of time, nor could she comprehend any of the Arabic being spoken around her.

At long last the beast came to a halt. At a shouted command it fell to one knee, and again rough hands grabbed her. Still in her cocoon, she was tossed over someone's shoulder.

Suddenly she was cast to the ground, where she freed herself from the loathsome blanket. At last she could see! She was in a tent, but it was a tent unlike anything she could have imagined. It was beautifully appointed with silken draperies and pillows and exotic palm frond decorations. There was a low mosaic table upon which sat an exquisite coffee urn made of copper and brass, along with trays of dates and nuts and fruits.

"Welcome, Miss Jacoby."

Jillian gasped. Seated upon an ebony chair was the man with the scarred face. He was staring at her with an unpleasant smile, his teeth very white against the darkness of his features.

Jillian struggled to her feet. Who in God's name was he, and what did he want from her?

"Welcome," he repeated, and his smile deepened in a way that chilled her to her bones as he stood and came toward her. It was a ruthless smile, and Jillian turned to run.

She stopped quickly. The entryway was blocked by two very large men with evil expressions, and long swords belted to their waists. She heard the laughter of the man with the scarred face behind her, and she swung around, praying for courage.

"This is kidnapping!" she snapped, trying to appear confident. "I don't know what you want from me, but I'm an American citizen, and you can't get away with this."

"Fine. Thank you for the warning. Now where is it, Miss Jacoby?"

"Where is what?" she demanded in genuine exasperation.

"The film. The film for Achmed Jabbar."

She stared at him blankly. "I don't have any film. Not for any Achmed Jabbar or anyone else! I don't

even know what you're talking about!'' She forced a
smile. ''Honest to God. I'd give you your film if I had
it, but I don't. So please, if you'll just get your goons
to move away, I'll leave. No hard feelings. I'll just
forget the whole thing. Now—oh!''

She broke off, screaming in sudden fear and pain.
He had caught her elbow and twisted it cruelly behind
her back. His menacing whisper just reached her ear.

''I can make you more cooperative, Miss Jacoby,
and I can enjoy every minute of it. You're a very
beautiful woman. All that blond hair and soft white
skin.''. He released her suddenly, shoving her away
from him with such force that she landed on the blanket. He smiled, stepping over to her again, pulling his
switchblade from a fold of his burnoose. ''It's American, too,'' he told her, indicating the blade. He turned
it in his hands and smiled. ''It can leave the most delicate ribbon of blood against your flesh—''

He broke off, because there was a sudden commo-
tion at the entryway. He turned away from her, his
burning gaze falling on the nervous newcomer, a
short, squat man who spoke very anxiously and
quickly. The man with the scarred face started to leave,
then turned back to Jillian.

''Excuse me. I promise I'll return as quickly as I
can,'' he said with cold menace. Then he left the tent,
his guards behind him. Jillian quickly ran to the entrance, only to discover that the guards had not gone
far. They greeted her effort with amusement, then
took her arms and deposited her less than graciously
on the blanket again.

Time passed slowly. Jillian alternately swore to
herself and fought the tears of panic that rose to her

eyes. She also ranted against Alex Montgomery. Somehow this was all his fault—she was sure of it.

Then she wished desperately that he were with her.

Darkness fell. There was no light in the tent, only whatever moonlight filtered through the translucent walls. Desolate and despairing, Jillian curled against one of the silken pillows, trying not to think of what might happen when her captor returned.

She was so exhausted that she started to doze, but then a slight flicker of movement caught her attention. She looked up. Silhouetted against the walls of the tent was the shadow of a man rising behind her. A scream caught in her throat, and she spun around, ready to do battle. Someone was coming toward her. Someone clothed in black from head to toe, moving silently, stealthily, toward her.

Suddenly he leaped forward and caught her, his hand swiftly covering her mouth.

"For God's sake, don't scream," a familiar voice whispered. "It's me!"

"Alex!"

"The same."

"Alex, you son of a—" she began, but her words faded away as she saw the relief—and the tenderness—in his eyes.

He smiled ruefully in the pale light. His thumbs brushed caressingly over her cheeks, and he asked tensely, "Did he hurt you?"

"No."

He lowered his head until his cheek rested against hers, then inhaled sharply. "I was so frightened for you. I'm going to kill that son of a bitch this time. If he had touched you . . ."

His voice trailed away, and he stared at her again with an emotion so intense that she felt as if she were melting. And then his lips met hers, and he kissed her with such passion that she actually forgot she'd been dragged into the desert and threatened with torture, and all because of some ridiculous roll of film she didn't even have. All she knew was the fever of his lips on hers, the sensual, sweeping stroke of his tongue, the hunger with which he touched her, and the sweet, desperate need he roused in her. She wanted him so badly. Her arms curled around his neck, and she wove her fingers through the hair at his nape, then felt the wonderful hot fusion of their bodies melding together. She felt ridiculously safe and secure, and deep in the recesses of her heart, she knew she was falling in love.

Love? How could she think about love? She was in this mess because of him.

Jillian twisted away from him, furious. "Damn you, Alex Montgomery! What in God's name is going on here?"

"I can't tell you now. We've got to get out of here. There's no time for explanations."

"Alex..."

But he was on his feet, as swift and agile as a black panther in the darkness. He laced his fingers through hers and pulled her along to the rear of the tent, where he had slashed an opening.

"You're no Egyptologist!" she whispered furiously.

"Yes, I am," he whispered back. "Now go!"

He shoved her through the opening, then followed close behind. She came out to a night alive with stars and a cooling breeze. In the distance she heard music and laughter, and she could see soft firelight outside a huge tent. She could hear camels braying and the snorts of horses, and smell the odors of sheep and goats.

"Let's go." Alex tugged on her hand. "Run. Now!"

She ran by his side, and together they reached a horse, a prancing, chestnut Arabian.

"Can you ride?" he asked.

"No!"

"Well, you're about to learn!" He swung her up, tossing her easily astride, then followed.

"Montgomery!"

The man with the scar was running toward them. But Alex didn't answer. Instead he dug his heels into the horse's flanks, and the Arabian reared, then galloped into the night.

Jillian turned to look behind them. Her hair flew across her face in the wind, nearly blinding her, and only Alex's embrace kept her on the horse, but she could see enough to be afraid. Scarface was now mounted, along with three others. And they were racing after Alex—after her—as they fled into the dark, never-ending void of the desert.

* * * * *

To be continued...
Join us next month, only in Silhouette Intimate Moments, for the next exciting installment of
SHADOWS ON THE NILE.

FOUR UNIQUE SERIES FOR EVERY WOMAN YOU ARE...

Silhouette Romance

Love, at its most tender, provocative, emotional...in stories that will make you laugh and cry while bringing you the magic of falling in love.

6 titles per month

Silhouette Special Edition

Sophisticated, substantial and packed with emotion, these powerful novels of life and love will capture your imagination and steal your heart.

6 titles per month

Silhouette Desire

Open the door to romance and passion. Humorous, emotional, compelling—yet always a believable and sensuous story—Silhouette Desire never fails to deliver on the promise of love.

6 titles per month

Silhouette Intimate Moments

Enter a world of excitement, of romance heightened by suspense, adventure and the passions every woman dreams of. Let us sweep you away.

4 titles per month

Take 4 Silhouette Special Edition novels
and a surprise gift
FREE

Then preview 6 brand-new books—delivered to your door as soon as they come off the presses! If you decide to keep them, you pay just $2.49 each*—a 9% saving off the retail price, *with no additional charges for postage and handling!*

Romance is alive, well and flourishing in the moving love stories of Silhouette Special Edition novels. They'll awaken your desires, enliven your senses and leave you tingling all over with excitement.

Start with 4 Silhouette Special Edition novels and a surprise gift absolutely FREE. They're yours to keep without obligation. You can always return a shipment and cancel at any time. Simply fill out and return the coupon today!

* Plus 69¢ postage and handling per shipment in Canada.

Silhouette Special Edition®

Clip and mail to: Silhouette Books

In U.S.:
901 Fuhrmann Blvd.
P.O. Box 9013
Buffalo, NY 14240-9013

In Canada:
P.O. Box 609
Fort Erie, Ontario
L2A 5X3

YES! Please rush me 4 free Silhouette Special Edition novels and my free surprise gift. Then send me 6 Silhouette Special Edition novels to preview each month as soon as they come off the presses. Bill me at the low price of $2.49 each*—a 9% saving off the retail price. There is no minimum number of books I must purchase. I can always return a shipment and cancel at any time. Even if I never buy another book from Silhouette Special Edition, the 4 free novels and surprise gift are mine to keep forever.
* Plus 69¢ postage and handling per shipment in Canada.

235 BPC BP7F

Name _____ (please print)

Address _____ Apt. _____

City _____ State/Prov. _____ Zip/Postal Code _____

This offer is limited to one order per household and not valid to present subscribers. Price is subject to change.   SE-SUB-1C

ATTRACTIVE, SPACE SAVING BOOK RACK

Display your most prized novels on this handsome and sturdy book rack. The hand-rubbed walnut finish will blend into your library decor with quiet elegance, providing a practical organizer for your favorite hard-or soft-covered books.

Only $9.95

**Approximately
16" x 8"
when assembled**

Assembles in seconds!

To order, rush your name, address and zip code, along with a check or money order for $10.70* ($9.95 plus 75¢ postage and handling) payable to *Silhouette Books*.

Silhouette Books
Book Rack Offer
901 Fuhrmann Blvd.
P.O. Box 1396
Buffalo, NY 14269-1396

Offer not available in Canada.

*New York and Iowa residents add appropriate sales tax.

BKR-2A

COMING NEXT MONTH

#225 STRANGERS IN PARADISE
—Heather Graham Pozzessere

Alexi came to Florida looking for peace and quiet. Instead, she found a house haunted by nighttime intruders. Her neighbor, Rex Morrow, was sure she needed protection, and her mind agreed, though her heart knew it would be much safer without Rex than with him.

#226 FANTASY MAN—Paula Detmer Riggs

Marshal Tatum Summers was falling in love with handsome Dan Kendall when she discovered he might not be as law-abiding as he seemed. She started investigating, determined to prove his innocence to the world, and just as determined to prove to him that they could have a future—together.

#227 WINDS OF FEAR—Margaret Malkind

Celine Conway had come to England on business, but she immediately found herself caught up in a whirlwind of adventure, intrigue and danger. Only Ian Evans seemed to know what was going on, but Celine wasn't sure she trusted him— though she knew she could easily love him.

#228 WHATEVER IT TAKES
—Patricia Gardner Evans

Sarah Harland thought Matthew Weston was her children's imaginary playmate, a substitute for the father they had lost. But Matthew was very real, as real as his love for Sarah—and as real as the dangerous secret he was keeping.

AVAILABLE THIS MONTH:

#221 SECRETS
Jennifer Greene

#222 EDGE OF THE WORLD
Kathleen Korbel

#223 EASY TARGET
Frances Williams

#224 DAY AND NIGHT
Maura Seger

BY DEBBIE MACOMBER....

ONCE UPON A TIME, in a land not so far away, there lived a girl, Debbie Macomber, who grew up dreaming of castles, white knights and princes on fiery steeds. Her family was an ordinary one with a mother and father and one wicked brother, who sold copies of her diary to all the boys in her junior high class.

One day, when Debbie was only nineteen, a handsome electrician drove by in a shiny black convertible. Now Debbie knew a prince when she saw one, and before long they lived in a two-bedroom cottage surrounded by a white picket fence.

As often happens when a damsel fair meets her prince charming, children followed, and soon the two-bedroom cottage became a four-bedroom castle. The kingdom flourished and prospered, and between soccer games and car pools, ballet classes and clarinet lessons, Debbie thought about love and enchantment and the magic of romance.

One day Debbie said, "What this country needs is a good fairy tale." She remembered how well her diary had sold and she dreamed again of castles, white knights and princes on fiery steeds. And so the stories of Cinderella, Beauty and the Beast, and Snow White were reborn....

Look for Debbie Macomber's *Legendary Lovers* trilogy from Silhouette Romance: *Cindy and the Prince* (January, 1988); *Some Kind of Wonderful* (March, 1988); *Almost Paradise* (May, 1988). Don't miss them!

SRT-1